Breach

A TERRIFYING SUMMER ADVENTURE

HOLLY S ROBERTS

Wicked Story Telling

WICKED STORY TELLING

Contents

Prologue

The small old boat jerked suddenly, a warning that almost went unheeded by the two teens absorbed in their laughter. As one teetered dangerously close to the edge, his friend's quick reflexes saved him from a plunge into the cold ocean.

Earlier that day, they had encountered a school of surfperch and effortlessly reached their fishing limit. Tossing their stringer of fish over the side to keep for their journey home, they spent the rest of their time relaxing, exchanging bad jokes, and planning their impending senior year dominance at high school. They had set out on their pre-summer fishing expedition as the sun graced the horizon, armed with bait, fishing gear, sandwiches, and a six-pack of beer pilfered by the younger teen from his father.

The unseasonably warm day with low clouds had promised early morning rain that never materialized. Having finished the beer and their overabundance of crude jokes, the boys were preparing for their return to shore about two hundred yards away. The setting sun glowed with a kaleidoscope of colors, but it was an unseen beauty because the teens' focus was now on the water. Realization struck that they should have moved closer to land at least an hour ago.

Neither was aware the delay would prove fatal.

"What the hell was that?" the older of the two by a few months demanded, his gaze scanning the now menacing waters. He was the serious one, good in school, always on time for football practice, and took out the garbage for his mom without being told. His friend was the exact opposite and could be counted on to be late and find sick humor in any mishap.

The boat jolted again and water poured through a weakened metal seam at the bottom.

The older teen's thoughts weren't dwelling on his brother, who had worked hard for three years before leaving for college to buy the seawater fishing boat. It didn't matter that the vessel was aged or relatively small for ocean fishing; it had still cost over ten grand.

No, his mind was fixated on what lurked beneath them. As the boat rocked, his eyes scanned the dark water with terror creeping into his thoughts. Panic set in as a massive gray fin sliced through the water, the unmistakable sign of a predator.

"Shark!" The cry, tinged with fear, marked a chilling realization of their vulnerability.

His friend pointed to the large gray fin emerging six feet off the starboard side that he had already seen. Even in the water's murky darkness, the shark's colossal size was clear—easily fifteen feet or larger.

"Great White," the older boy muttered as his brain kicked into gear.

"Look!" the other teen pointed again; his body now facing the opposite direction.

A similar fin surfaced on the port side. The older boy's gaze darted sharply from side to side, questioning whether there were two sharks or if the one had moved with astonishing speed.

He started the motor while assessing the distance to shore. The engine cranked over immediately, offering a glimmer of hope. When they had embarked on their adventure that morning, the engine had struggled until it warmed up. It was their first fishing trip of the season, a tradition to mark the end of their high school year two weeks before summer officially began. The uncertain weather forecast had kept most recreational boats ashore, providing them with the solitude they looked for.

With the next hit, directly below the boat, the bow lifted, and the twelve-foot craft took on more water.

"Hold on," the older boy urged. He hit the throttle, propelling them forward.

"Wahoo!" his friend exclaimed in excitement as they gained speed, heading toward the shoreline. "We showed that bitch who's boss."

The older teen took in a deep breath, exhaling slowly as the tension melted from his shoulders, allowing a tentative smile. Saltwater spray kissed his face, and nothing had ever felt so invigorating. This would be the fishing story that defined their senior year.

The boat went airborne and flipped.

Their screams were cut short. The water churned and the blood dissipated within minutes.

The sharks moved on.

Two weeks later (if you didn't read the prologue, go back)

K ate, dressed in dark blue shorts and a white gauzy blouse, her hair piled in a messy bun, glanced at her five-year-old daughter, Ryan, and beckoned her over with a quick motion of her finger.

"Turn around; let's check your backpack for the iPad," Kate said as her husband, Sam, completed a final round to secure the house.

"I checked Mom. It's there," Ryan said while pivoting on her small white deck shoes with a scowl that showed she was past ready to leave.

"You're right—it's here," Kate confirmed, her fingers brushing against the purple rubber case amidst the backpack's contents of items only a young girl would accumulate.

"We're all set," announced Sam, stepping into the living room from the rear of the house.

"Can we leave now?" implored Ryan, her short brown curls bouncing with each impatient shift from foot to foot.

She had woken before sunrise, placed her favorite grandpop gift around her neck, donned her new pristine white marine clothes, which had colorful dolphins and sea turtles strategically placed around the hems of the shirt and shorts, and was ready to go before Kate's blurry eyes could focus. Ryan had posed her question about leaving every fifteen minutes during breakfast and their departure preparations.

"Let's do this," Sam agreed, smiling at Kate.

"Yay!" Ryan exclaimed, jumping up and down on both feet instead of alternating.

Kate scooped up her red backpack from the floor, settling it on her lap.

"Need a hand with that?" Sam offered.

"Nope, I'm ready," she replied with a firm cast to her lips because she hated being treated like an invalid even if she felt like one most days.

Gripping the wheels, Kate pivoted her chair towards the door and rolled forward. Her excitement built as the steady hum of the van's lift positioned her wheelchair, and Sam secured it in place with a downward push on the levers.

Eighteen months had passed since the accident that left her with an incomplete spinal cord injury, taking away the use of her legs. The rehabilitation center staff had believed her fortunate for retaining some sensation below the waist, but Kate had never felt unluckier.

She'd gone through the five stages of grief; denial, anger, bargaining, depression and finally acceptance. Acceptance was still the hardest and some days she took a backwards step into depression again. Kate shrugged her unhappy thoughts aside. The yachting adventure was a step toward healing that she'd needed over the past year and finally, it was happening.

Six months since settling with the other driver's insurance had allowed them to adapt their newly purchased 61-foot yacht for wheelchair access. The modifications were completed a week before and they'd used the time before their departure to stock it with what was needed for a month's voyage. They were fortunate that one of her father's friends had sold them the yacht at a steal. They'd christened it Ryan's Gift in a small private ceremony the night before.

Kate's father, Dr. Greg Sawyer, a marine biologist who worked currently out of the San Francisco Bay, had been teaching Sam to handle the yacht alone. In his seventies, Greg had no intention of retiring and hoped to spend his final years at sea. He trusted his daughter on sea and land, but even with the modifications to the yacht, Sam had to be able to handle the beast alone.

They would reunite with Kate's father a few weeks into their maiden voyage to allow Ryan to spend time with him. Kate had little doubt that her daughter would follow in her grandpop's footsteps, despite Kate pursuing a different path.

Kate and Sam met in college and married shortly after graduation. They entered the business finance world and worked hard for the things that were important to them. Three years later, they had bought a home and started their one-child family. Kate gave up her career for a few years to pour herself into motherhood. Life went as planned until three months before her accident. For the first time, her marriage hit a devastating rough spot.

Again, Kate had to shove aside the gloomy thoughts that brought such mental turmoil, at times making it hard to breathe. It didn't help that she and Sam rarely spoke of their rocky marriage prior to the accident.

Darn, this was not the time to allow melancholy to dog her steps.

The thought coaxed a smile and a headshake from Kate. Steps or wheels, as long as she could move from point A to B, she would be thankful. And she would keep telling herself that until she believed it. She hated how easily her thoughts pulled her down and she was determined to change her perspective during the voyage. She wanted the old Kate back.

She turned her head and observed the roadside landscape while Ryan watched a movie in the backseat. Their destination was the Chula Vista Marina, in San Diego, an hour drive on Interstate 5 if traffic kept flowing.

A familiar warm hand grasped her fingers, squeezing slightly. Regardless of their troubled marriage, Sam had been her rock since the accident. She turned her smile toward him and reciprocated the squeeze. He was a good-looking thirty-four-year-old man with curly, short-cropped, medium brown hair the same shade as his daughter's. Sam's large green eyes and provocative smile always brought her up short when he turned them her way, and even with the unrest she felt, his good cheer was hard to resist.

"There's the ocean," he said as the highway curved, offering them their first view of the day. Ryan was too engrossed in her movie to hear him.

Kate's heartbeat accelerated as she glanced at the choppy blue water. The ocean's expanse beckoned, a vast canvas for her family's story to unfold, each wave a reminder of the strength and perseverance needed to navigate the journey ahead.

TWO YEARS BEFORE...

"She's down, what's so important we had to have an official family meeting?" Kate asked Sam with a cheeky grin. Their daughter was smart, but they could usually talk around her comprehension level for minor things. Sam's serious expression took her good cheer away.

"Sam?"

The look of devastation in his eyes was not what she expected. Was he ill? Did he have cancer?

"Sam, you're scaring me," she said desperately.

"I love you," he replied softly. "I've loved you since the first time I saw you."

Their relationship had been a whirlwind courtship. So many people didn't believe in love at first sight, but they were the unlucky ones. The moment Beth laid eyes on Sam, she knew he was the one.

"I love you too. Now stop torturing me and tell me what's up."

He took her hand and then released it.

"It's a woman I work with. I did something I can't take back."

The jumble of words flowing inside her brain didn't make sense.

"A woman?"

"She means nothing. I was stupid and I can't tell you how sorry I am. The guilt has been eating me alive."

He looked at her as if she should feel good about the guilt but she was still trying to make sense of what he'd said—A woman at work. He did something he can't take back. The growing knot in her stomach clenched tighter. Her vision darkened around the edges.

"You had sex with her?" It came out so soft because her throat choked up. This couldn't be happening.

"I'm sorry, I can't begin to tell you how much."

The anger began setting in and Beth's vision came back into focus. Her husband, the man she loved, the father of her child, the person she'd given her life to. Sam cheated. If a horse kicked her upside the head, she couldn't be more shocked.

"You need to understand that it meant nothing. It happened, it's over with, and I'm willing to do anything, even go to therapy."

"You slept with another woman and you're willing to go to therapy?"

"Yes, anything," he said and went to his knees in front of her and took her hands.

They were warm whereas hers were ice cold. Everything that made her happy had just collapsed. No, that wasn't true. They had a beautiful daughter. They. There was no they. Sam cheated.

"Why?" she asked, pulling her hands from his, his touch burning.

"It was stupid. A mistake. It meant no—." The look in Beth's eyes brought him up short.

"You slept with another woman and it meant nothing. Is that supposed to make me feel better?" Her voice had risen. Ryan, Kate couldn't forget she was sleeping down the hall. Her world had collapsed but she had to be sure her daughter was protected.

"Get out," she said to the man she'd loved for years.

"Beth. I'm sorry. I'll do anything."

"You'll get out. Go somewhere. A hotel. Or to that woman. Just leave."

"You don't mean that. I know you're angry—." Again the look she gave him made him stop speaking.

"I'll be in the guest room until you're gone," she said, rising. "Pack your things and leave."

She walked down the hall and closed the door behind her. She didn't cry though she knew that would come eventually. For now, she was numb, completely dead inside. As she stood there, the shock and disbelief faded and still she couldn't reconcile the reality of Sam's betrayal. He'd smashed the trust and love she thought they shared. The guest room was their joint home office. Beth went to the floor, crumbling beneath the weight of his deception. She curled into a tight ball and still there were no tears.

Her sadness was more like grief. She didn't just mourn the loss of their relationship, she mourned the loss of their future. Self-doubt surfaced, and she questioned everything about her life. Had Sam cheated because he was unfulfilled in their marriage?

Confusion took over. She was torn between the love she still felt and the pain of Sam's betrayal. The first tear fell.

*

Four months later...

The meeting at work had gone longer than Beth expected. Sam had picked Ryan up from daycare, thank goodness. Beth pulled into traffic while thinking about what she would make Ryan for dinner. The child loved SpaghettiOs but she'd had it the night before and Beth knew it held little nutritional value.

Sam wanted to come home, but Beth wasn't ready. Working full-time and being a single mother kicked her butt and Sam knew it. He simply waited for her to cave so they could go back to a happy marriage. A marriage that she would never trust again.

The car beside her veered heavily to the left and Beth turned slightly just in time to see the semi-truck running the red light. The crunch of metal, pain, and the smell of gasoline was all she remembered days later when they brought her out of the drug-induced coma.

There was one other thing she remembered. Her husband betrayed her.

RYAN'S GIFT, DAY ONE

Kate maneuvered her wheelchair up the ramp with a practiced ease that belied the turmoil beneath her calm exterior. Each push against the wheels was a silent testament to her resilience, a battle fought and won against the confines of her new reality. Her upper body strength had significantly improved during months of rehabilitation and continued efforts afterward. Despite her dislike for the chair, she was determined not to let it impede her progress.

The pains she had endured in the first year, stemming from the spinal injury, had largely dissipated, and she hadn't taken painkillers in months. She carried them just in case but doubted their necessity. A glass of wine typically sufficed to alleviate the minor discomforts often overlooked by those not using a wheelchair.

Adapting to a world designed for individuals of average height proved frustrating for Kate. Simply going to the grocery store where everything she needed seemed to be out of reach was beyond annoying. She was overcharged on her last visit and the counter, where she'd gone to get a refund, was made for standing individuals. It made her invisible and the list went on and on. Nevertheless, she had adjusted and remained committed to finding peace in her new world.

The yacht had undergone thoughtful modifications, featuring low counters in the galley, ramped walkways and a chair lift with backup ropes for navigating below deck. A custom wheelchair awaited her there too and would be used solely on the lower level.

The individual responsible for these upgrades was a genius, evident in the addition of a rail around the outer deck to prevent accidents in rough seas. The master berth now housed a luxury shower accessible to Kate in her wheelchair. The yacht, tailored to accommodate her unique sitting height, provided a comforting environment. Even the subtle pitch below her chair calmed her. With a deep inhale that filled her lungs with saltwater air, she allowed her stress to fade.

Ryan's berth had also been reconstructed to cater to a curious five-year-old fascinated by science and water. The space now included a desk and a secure stand for her iPad, so she could communicate with her grandpop whenever he was available.

Sam, having brought in the last of their luggage, engaged in conversation with Dan, the port steward, who provided last-minute updates on weather and tides. The two had developed a rapport since leasing the slip for Ryan's Gift, and Dan had generously shared his extensive boating knowledge.

Before leaving port, Kate took a moment to call her dad and inform him of their imminent departure.

"Great to hear from you," Greg said. "Check in daily and give me an update of your coordinates so I can keep track."

Kate suppressed a groan. Her father's protective nature was both endearing and at times exasperating.

"The yacht is rigged so I can handle it if need be, and you know it," she assured him. He remained silent. "Daily updates it is. Love you, Dad, and we'll see you in a few weeks."

"That's my girl," he replied, his relief palpable.

Having sent her father away a month after the accident, Kate reflected on his persistent concern, recognizing it as an expression of love. They ended their call and she rolled back on deck as Dan helped Sam untie the lines from the cleats.

"We're the sendoff crew!" Bradon, Dan's ten-year-old son, yelled with excitement from the dock as he stood beside his mom who wore a huge smile.

Kate called inside for Ryan to join her, and soon, the stuffed, toy shark-wielding five-year-old emerged. Dan bid Sam farewell, leaping to the dock to stand with his family.

Sam, heading to the control room inside the upper cabin, demonstrated proficiency in navigating the yacht out of its berth. The sky was clear and the day warming up as they embarked on a three-week journey to the San Francisco Bay. Kate breathed in the sea air as she secured her long blonde hair with an elastic band from her wrist, feeling a thrill run across her bare arms as she looked out at the open water and took another deep breath.

"Mom," do you think grandpop will take me diving?" Ryan asked, clutching the tiger shark tooth hanging from her neck.

"If you brush your teeth each night without being told, he just might."

"Mooom," came the exaggerated wail. "Grandpop won't know if I brush my teeth."

Ryan always had a witty comeback, a trait she likely inherited from Beth, leaving little room for complaint.

"A little sea bird will tell him, I promise," said Kate.

"Does the sea bird's name start with K?" Ryan's small hands were at her waist. It was her, "I'm serious and want an answer," pose.

"Smarty," Kate said with a grin. "Come on, we have things to unpack and situate. Once that's done we can make plans for the rest of the day.

They put away the items that needed a home and settled in the galley, Kate's favorite place on board. She watched Sam at the controls, steering the yacht into open water. He'd come so far from his land loving days in a very short amount of time, or so it seemed.

Their discussions about refurbishing a yacht hadn't gone well in the beginning. With Kate's accident money, Sam didn't need to work. He had cut back on his time in the office and worked mostly from home. Kate wasn't sure if that was good or bad.

She remembered the final discussion before he gave into the ocean adventure idea.

"I feel stifled," she'd told him. Hurt filled his expression and she'd had to grit her teeth. "You don't understand," she added. "I need to feel the wind that sweeps in from the sea, and smell the scent of salt and the faint, briny aroma of ocean water."

He'd stared at her, still not understanding. "A boat won't stifle you more?" he'd asked.

"Once we're out of the bay, there's nothing but space."

"Okay," he finally agreed.

The whirlwind of preparations began the following day and started with a call to her father to find them a yacht. He had the connections they needed and two weeks later, it was delivered to the new berth at Chula Vista Marina.

As Kate sat looking outside, the relief she felt overshadowed her misgivings. Her father taught her early in life that the ocean healed.

"Can I go to the deck and watch for dolphins?" Ryan asked, bringing Kate out of her morose thoughts.

"That sounds like a great idea. We can look for sea turtles and stingrays too."

Within a few minutes they were settled on the deck chairs watching the ocean and enjoying the sea spray on their faces. Kate saw Ryan gently squeeze the shark tooth that hung around her neck. The past two years had seen so much turmoil with Ryan caught in the middle. This trip would heal the three of them.

The farther they traveled from land, the glassier the water. Kate looked into its infinite depths and a shiver passed over her skin.

DAY TWO

K ate awoke, ready for the new day. She'd left her clothes from the day before on the nightstand by her bed before she'd gone to sleep. After removing her nightgown, she pulled on her swimsuit top followed by a shirt before tackling the bottom half of her suit and the shorts. What once took under a minute, was now a reminder of all she'd lost. Bending at the waist, she manually lifted her left leg with her hand and tugged the swimsuit bottoms over her foot and repeated it on the other leg. Next came the fun part where she wiggled about as she moved the material beneath her butt and could pull them up, basically a fish flopping on dry land. Once the swimsuit was on, she moved to the shorts and repeated the entire process.

Winded after the dressing aerobics, she moved to the wheelchair and rolled to the sink in the bathroom. Here, she thoroughly appreciated the ability to move her wheelchair beneath the counter to brush her teeth and run a comb through her hair. She added a large amount of sunblock to her pale skin and hoped the sun would be kind until her flesh darkened. Everything was located at the perfect height. The small things mattered since her accident and the yacht made her feel more self-sufficient.

At the short stairwell, Kate moved from her wheelchair to the lift and hit the button that took her to the upper deck where her topside wheel-chair waited. She knew she was fortunate to have the financial means to accommodate her disability, but it didn't lower her resentment that she was living in a nightmare that wasn't her fault.

Positive thoughts, Kate reminded herself silently.

She had successfully prepared and served their first substantial meal on board the night before, and she pulled on that sense of accomplishment. She and Sam had shared a bottle of wine before retiring to their separate berths—not an ideal situation, but part of the challenges they faced since his infidelity.

Their attempts at intimacy since Kate's recovery had been unsuc-cessful. Despite being in good enough condition, she struggled to ar-ticulate her true feelings. Her psychologist had made her aware that the primary hurdle lay within herself. Kate had not forgiven Sam and she wasn't sure she could. She was also on uneven grounds in the marriage because she could no longer take care of herself. It all added up to the biggest question. Why had he cheated and destroyed what she thought of as a solid marriage? She still didn't have answers and she wasn't sure she could handle them now.

Sam had moved back home to care for Ryan immediately after the accident. He stayed when Kate returned from six months in rehab. A month after returning home, an impacted bowel led to an elevated temperature and an emergency room visit that extended into a three-day hospital stay. Sam handled the situation with composure, displaying no signs of disgust, but Kate couldn't shake her own sense of revulsion.

Monitoring her daily bathroom habits closely had proved futile, leading to the embarrassing hospital procedure that she barely remembered due to her high temperature. Sam had witnessed her at her most vulnerable.

Before the accident, they were an unhappy couple dealing with Sam's admission. Although deeply repentant, his infidelity had initially felt like an insurmountable betrayal. She thought their marriage was over. Then the situation changed for everyone. Forgiveness was still difficult to contemplate. Sam's unfaithfulness hit her on a level she was unsure she could climb down from. Her anger and grief over what he'd done hadn't settled and their new circumstances gave her too much to think about and some days she simply wanted to never see him again. She had to find a way to come to terms with his betrayal and make good decisions for her and Ryan.

Shaking off the irritation her thoughts caused, she finished stowing the breakfast dishes and wheeled herself onto the deck, where Sam and Ryan waited. Kate drank in the ocean air and the beautiful scenery that she hadn't realized she craved so much.

To most children her childhood would seem idyllic. While others sat in a classroom, Kate spent weeks at sea, documenting her father's findings as soon as she was old enough to write. He was her teacher in everything from reading to arithmetic and history. She aced the homeschool tests and thought her entire life would follow that of her fathers.

Her teenage years hit and for the first time Kate was lonely for friends her own age. She wanted to be a normal girl and do normal things. Though her father understood her heart's yearning, it was hard for him to change but he did. Greg enrolled her in public school and watched from the sidelines as her life course altered and the water no longer held such fascination. He'd never told her anything but how proud he was of her accomplishments.

She missed him but in a few weeks she would see him again. With that thought firmly in place, she turned to her husband and daughter.

Having anchored offshore overnight, Sam had navigated them into deeper waters when he first woke up. Land was barely visible, and they were anchored again to work off their breakfast. On the casting deck at the bow, Kate's exercise mat was rolled out and waiting. The casting deck's height allowed her to transition from the wheelchair to the mat easily, and Ryan, her workout coach, was ready for the morning routine.

"You need to work extra hard today," Ryan said excitedly.

"And why is that?" Kate asked with a grin.

"Grandpop said the routine set on the first day at sea preps you for the entire voyage," Ryan replied like she was teaching a great life lesson.

Kate knew the answer but wanted her daughter to feel important in aiding with her physical therapy. Ryan was the best cheerleader a paraplegic could ask for.

Kate stretched out on the mat and laid back. Ryan lifted her right leg with a small endearing grunt, and worked her hip joint with abduction, adduction, outward rotation and inward rotation movements.

"Discomfort?" Ryan asked in an adult tone before she moved on to Kate's knee.

She had attended most of the physical therapy sessions with Kate so she could learn how to help her mom. With all the attention on Kate after the accident, Ryan needed a sense of purpose in her mother's recovery and they found it in exercise.

"Nope, it feels good," Kate replied, though she felt little.

Ryan lifted Kate's leg so the knee bent and started working flexion and extensions. The entire routine took forty-five minutes per leg and Ryan was often too tired to do both sides. The exercises involved stretching, hip joint movements, and knee, ankle, and toe flexion and extensions of which Kate could not do on her own. With the help of Sam and Ryan, she had a little sensation in the big toe of her right foot. For her it was a miracle but the doctors had not been hopeful. On the other hand, her physical therapist, Roxy, gave her the pep talk she held onto.

"In the scheme of things, there's a lot unknown about spinal cord injuries. Miracles happen so don't give up." It was advice Kate held onto even though she knew her outcome was dismal.

Sam watched the physical therapy routine in the background, green eyes covered by dark aviators, holding his stainless steel water bottle. Dressed in tan board shorts and a white polo shirt, he couldn't hide how attractive he was. Resentment surfaced momentarily, but Kate pushed it away, reminding herself that the other woman in their marriage was long gone.

She took time to admire her husband's brown wavy hair that ruffled softly in the breeze. Ridiculous jealousy sparked again until he took over her left side therapy. She could never think badly of him when he was helping her stay healthy.

While he worked, Ryan sat beside them chatting excitedly about the day ahead.

"I'm recording water temperatures for Grandpop and I'm keeping a list of the ocean life we see," Ryan told them.

Kate remembered doing the exact same things for her father that Ryan was doing. Greg's expertise revolved around stingrays which were the love of his career. She would sit next to him at night while he transferred her findings into his main logbook. He would make her feel like she was an important part of his research. He was there for Ryan too and Kate was grateful.

After they completed the workout, Kate moved back into her wheelchair, and followed her family to the stern to use the platform for a dip in the ocean. Swimming had become Kate's sanctuary after realizing she might never walk again. Water provided weightlessness and allowed her to recall the time before the accident. She wheeled herself to the casting platform and shimmied out of her shorts and shirt. Sam helped her get situated so she could sit with her legs in the water.

Wearing a colorful two-piece bikini, Kate entered the ocean with Sam and Ryan jumping in behind her. They swam laps around Ryan's Gift while Kate enjoyed the feel of the cool water against her skin.

"Look, Mom," Ryan called out, waving her hand excitedly—dolphins, six in total, one a small juvenile.

Her grandpops told her that seeing wildlife in the ocean was a positive sign and Ryan held onto his every word. If he said it, whatever it was, was written in stone. Kate understood. She behaved exactly as her daughter when she was young.

Kate called her father weekly. His professed horrors about the dying oceans grew exponentially worse each time they spoke. It saddened her that his life work to understand stingrays, was now eaten away by his advocacy for the planet's oceans and seas.

"What kind are they?" Kate asked, deciding to give her daughter a check to see what her grandpops had taught her.

"Bottlenose," Ryan replied. "Look, there's a baby. It's so sweet. I want a stuffed dolphin to go with my stuffed shark."

"Name the types of dolphins in this area," Kate prompted. "If you get them correct, I'll buy you the stuffed dolphin."

"That's easy," Ryan said while treading water and holding up her fingers one at a time as she named them, "Bottlenose, Specific White-Sided"—the correct word was "Pacific," but Kate didn't correct her—"Common dolphin, and Risso's dolphin."

"Good job," Kate said as she too admired the baby.

The dolphins were mesmerizing with their grace and camaraderie. They moved with remarkable coordination, their sleek bodies slicing through the water with effortless agility. The sunlight caught on their wet skin, making it glisten and shimmer against the contrasting blue. Kate had always loved their synchronized movements and social interactions, from gentle nudging to spirited chases, their complex relationships within a pod had fascinated her for years. The sounds of their clicks and whistles add an auditory layer to the spectacle they were currently witnessing. They offered a harmonious blend of freedom, intelligence, and social connection, and were a testament to the wonders of marine life.

The playful dolphins approached, curious yet keeping a slight distance to protect the young one. It was a spectacular sighting for their first day.

When the dolphins swam away, Kate took another lap because she was growing cold. It didn't help as she needed so she left the water and went inside to take a warm shower.

It felt good to be alive.

DAY THREE

Kate hummed as she prepared their second breakfast onboard. Wearing a light blue gauzy dress that allowed her body to breathe in the rising warmth of the day, she couldn't believe how much she enjoyed cooking in the custom galley. When they returned home, she would start their kitchen remodel as soon as possible.

Unless you were confined to a wheeled world, people had no concept of how difficult the most basic life necessities could be. The first time she tried to brush her teeth in her bathroom, the chair wouldn't get her close enough to the sink and she ended up spitting in the garbage can and then crying because it hadn't occurred to her to bring a cup into the bathroom. The simple things that she had never considered were always the ones that brought on strong emotions.

"Dammit," Sam exclaimed, breaking into her wandering thoughts, a second after the galley lights went out.

"Dad, language," Ryan chided, without looking up from her coloring book.

It made Kate smile. Both she and Sam tried not to swear in front of their daughter, but Sam had occasional slip-ups, and Ryan had no problem keeping him in line.

Kate glanced at the electrical lights in the control room; they were out as well. Because the yacht was older, they had hired an electrician to go through it and rewire sections for the extras they had installed. Maybe they should have had it thoroughly checked again before the voyage.

"I'll take a look," Sam said, grabbing a small toolbox from one of the storage compartments below the dinette seat and heading to the electrical room. He had stripped down to colorful board shorts he planned to swim in later. He hadn't bothered shaving, and the scruff gave him a rugged appearance.

Even though he looked the part, Kate grinned at seeing him with the toolbox. Sam was not a handyman, and Kate, having grown up on vessels that sometimes barely ran, was accustomed to the occasional mishap. She'd helped bail water for hours on one of the trips with her father when she was young, and their pump went out. During another adventure, she'd handed tools to Greg while he worked on an old engine that gave out a week into their stingray breeding behavior expedition. She looked back at it now as good times.

Within ten minutes, power was restored, and Kate resumed cooking breakfast.

"The inverter shut down," Sam explained in exasperation upon returning to the galley, hoisting the toolbox onto the table, and sitting beside Ryan. "I changed the fuse, and it started back up. We'll have it looked at when we meet up with pops."

Ryan's Gift had four solar panels and a wind generator for most of their onboard power needs. The electrician had warned them about the yacht's aging generator, which Greg had a replacement for once they rendezvoused.

"That's odd," Kate remarked. "We'll need to see if it happens again. Maybe we're overloading the circuit."

Sam shrugged. "Could be. We knew this would be an interesting first voyage."

She agreed. It had been over two years since Kate visited her father and he took her out to sea. That had only been for a single afternoon. The excursion had reminded Kate how much she loved the water. It was sad that it took a devastating accident to bring her back to the place she had called home for so many years.

"Ready to eat?" Kate asked, switching her thoughts to food. She'd prepared bacon and eggs with wholewheat toast. Sam had picked up a jar of their favorite strawberry preserves at the farmer's market, which added the perfect complement to the meal.

Sam stood and carried over the plates and bowls filled with their breakfast while Kate situated her wheelchair. With calm seas, locking it into place wasn't necessary, but she liked the feeling that it wouldn't move if they hit a few large waves, so she secured it.

"Yum, strawberry jam," Ryan exclaimed excitedly and grabbed a piece of toast as her father pushed the preserves in her direction. Before taking her first bite, Ryan looked at Kate. "Did you go poop this morning?" she asked.

"Not at the table," Kate replied, with a touch of color heating her cheeks. The hospital stay due to the impacted bowel was still too fresh, and she felt humiliated that Sam had been in the thick of the treatment to save her life. She needed to get over it, but their relationship was too undefined for her to feel comfortable about something so personal.

"It's my job," Ryan insisted. "You told me I had to help, and that's what I'm doing."

Kate wanted to hit her head against the table. She knew the question shouldn't bother her, but it embarrassed her in the worst possible way. Maybe her marriage was over, and she simply needed to face it.

"Thank you for your diligence," she told her daughter. "Yes, I did, and I logged it, no pun intended. Now it's time to eat without talking about bathroom behavior."

"What's a pun?" her daughter asked.

Sam laughed and shook his head. "She takes after your father, and it's too late to stop her now," he said.

Ryan looked indignant then grinned.

"I love grandpop, and I want to be just like him," she said earnestly.

"Eat," Kate said in mock sternness, hoping the bathroom talk was over.

"Eye, eye captain," Ryan said and added a salute that was too cute not to smile at.

"Aye, aye," her father corrected.

"What's an aye?" Ryan asked after taking a bite of eggs from her overfilled plate.

Kate was grateful to Sam for intervening and changing the focus of Ryan's never ending curiosity. She was inquisitive about everything, and her questions never stopped. Sometimes Kate or Sam had the answer, and sometimes they hit Google to satisfy their five-year-old's curiosity. She never asked the same question twice and could recite every fact she learned by storing them in her forever-stretching child's brain. She definitely came from her grandpop's bloodline.

"It's an old nautical term that means, yes," Kate told her.

"What she said," Sam nodded toward Kate.

"The pirates are saying 'yes, yes?'" Ryan asked skeptically.

Sam's expression turned hard, and his voice lowered. "If you want to be keelhauled for insubordination, try my patience again, matey."

"What's a keelhaul?" Ryan asked after a small bout of giggling at her father's silliness.

Kate groaned good-naturedly, and Sam winked at his daughter.

"It was a horrible punishment for men who defied their captain at sea," he said. "They were dragged by a rope beneath the keel of the ship, and it was very dangerous. Now eat your food so we can get today started."

They finished breakfast, stowed everything in its place, and did a few chores until their food settled. When they were ready, they moved to the outside deck to repeat the prior day's physical therapy.

The morning continued to grow warmer, but it still had a ways to go before the true summer heat set in. The further offshore they traveled, the more the sea gave relief with a cool breeze. Land was far behind them, and Kate sucked in the ocean air, happy to be back on the water. She lifted her hand and blocked the sun from her eyes as she appreciated the clear blue view of both water and sky.

When she finished absorbing the beauty, she moved from the wheelchair to the casting deck. She swung her body around, dragging her legs so she could steer them into the water.

Kate gave a small gasp and froze.

Six feet off the bow, a great white shark had its massive upper body above the water with two dark eyes looking straight at her. Kate knew the eyes were actually a dark blue but right now they looked black. There had been no splash or any other indicator that the predator was in the area.

"Mom," Ryan said nervously.

"I see it, honey," Kate replied. Great whites were one of a few ocean species that lifted their head above the water to look around for prey or sometimes out of simple curiosity.

"See what?" asked Sam, who was moving the wheelchair to the side so he could stand in his exercise observation spot. "Oh!" he said when he looked up.

"It's a great white," Kate replied, sounding calm when she felt exactly the opposite. Its colossal jaws with rows of teeth that could eat through steel should give anyone pause. It continued staring and then, with no sound and what seemed to be no displacement of water, it sank beneath the surface like it had never been there. Shivers ran along Kate's skin, but she kept her smile in place.

Sharks were the stingray's closest relative, so by default, Kate was familiar with sharks. She'd gone diving with them many times and actually touched a giant hammerhead when she was a teenager. Like her father, she preferred stingrays.

"I don't think we'll be swimming here this morning," Sam said.

Ryan jumped up and down and pumped her hand. Kate grabbed her ankle so she didn't fall overboard.

"I can add a great white shark to my logbook," Ryan said with true excitement. "Grandpop will love it." She peered over the side, making Kate stretch her arms and hold a bit tighter.

"Sharks are not the mean, fierce eating machines that Hollywood makes them into, but they are dangerous," she told her daughter. "What that shark did is called spy-hopping. They either spy with just an eye above the water line or they lift the upper part of their body above the surface so they can see farther like that one did."

"Why do they do it?" Ryan asked.

"Curiosity or looking for a meal," Kate said. "Scientists believe they also do it to scent the air for large carcasses floating on the surface." She shrugged. "Killer whales and dolphins do it too."

"I don't want to be a shark meal," Ryan said and looked a little more skeptically at the area where the shark disappeared. "It had a lot of big teeth."

"They're sharp too," Kate told her. "They have three rows, and when a front tooth falls out, another moves in and takes its place. Humans only grow two sets of teeth, their baby ones and their adult ones. Great white sharks grow teeth throughout their life."

Sam grabbed his daughter around the waist and physically moved her closer to Kate. Ryan wore her swim top and a pair of yellow shorts. Kate had slathered sunblock on her this morning, though Ryan's skin was tanned from playing outside.

"You ladies do your exercises, and I'll keep watch for sharks," Sam said. "If worst comes to worst, we'll feed it roast from the freezer. Ryan would be nothing more than a light snack," he teased.

He hid it, but Kate saw the worry in his expression. Sam hadn't grown up on the water, and he'd told her before that sharks were not his favorite marine animal. She'd replied that he just needed to hang out with her dad for a while, and he would change his mind. He'd done what she asked, but his unease over sharks and other large fish with sharp teeth remained. They would be lucky if he went back into the water during this voyage.

"I would be the shark's yummy dessert," his daughter said cheekily.

"Let's not test it," Sam said. He watched nervously as Ryan went through the physical therapy steps. "We'll pull anchor when you're done," he added.

The water remained calm, and the shark was probably long gone, but Kate didn't say it aloud. Seeing a great white so close and the silence of the animal literally lifting the top part of its body entirely out of the water spooked her too.

The main reason sharks were attracted to boats was for a meal. Either a bundle of caught fish hanging over the side in the water, or guides chumming the water to attract sharks for sightseers. Both situations caused problems.

Her thoughts returned to the shark she'd just seen. Kate would swear it stared at her with menace.

Top of Form

DAY THREE, EVENING

Sam entered the galley after finishing Ryan's favorite bedtime story. He'd showered and dressed in cotton pants and a comfortable T-shirt with the slogan, "I'm a girl dad." It had been a Father's Day gift from Ryan, and he loved it. Still unshaven, he was looking more like a pirate with every passing hour. Kate wished she didn't find him so attractive; it wasn't helping the situation.

Kate had showered too. She'd changed into a long nightshirt that was a size too big, just the way she liked it. She felt drained, but in a good way, and for that, she was grateful.

Sam selected a bottle of red wine from the cabinet, bringing it and two glasses to the table where Kate sat. These times were the toughest for Kate. During the day, Ryan acted as a buffer between them, but at night, Kate couldn't escape the looming issues stemming from Sam's infidelity. Her resentment seemed to grow when they were alone.

"Do you think that shark will follow the boat?" Sam asked, pouring them both a glass.

Kate shook her head, suppressing a chuckle and an eye roll. "No, it was just curious. We don't fish, so there's really nothing we have to attract it. We're close to great white nursery territory. Maybe it gave birth or is heading there. If it's male, it might be looking to mate. I couldn't see enough to check for claspers. We'll never know." What Kate did know was that only one great white baby was recorded possibly directly after its birth but this had not been validated by the scientists who studied great whites. Overall they knew next to nothing about shark childbearing and mating habits. Mostly her reply was to keep Sam from worrying.

"Didn't that scare you?" He asked incredulously.

"It startled me," she said without admitting how anxious the shark made her feel. "I have a healthy respect for sharks, but I'm not worried it will follow the boat. Even if it's hungry, there's easier prey out there."

Sam took a hefty swallow from his glass. "Just so you know, I plan on having nightmares tonight."

Kate laughed, a rare moment of joy when it was just her and Sam alone.

"I miss that sound," Sam said sadly. "I miss you."

These conversations were painful, and she hoped to escape without feeling guilty.

"No matter how hard I try," she said, "I can never wrap my head around the why."

Sam had never given her a satisfying answer. To make it worse, he only told her because the other woman made waves when he broke it off. Sam had wanted Kate to hear the truth from him. If the other woman wouldn't have balked, Kate would have remained blissfully ignorant. She wished she had.

A part of Kate died the evening he told her. She'd thought they had a great marriage. They were friends too and did so much together including raising their daughter. Sam hadn't just cheated on her, he'd cheated on his family.

Sam ran his hand through his hair, staring at her with a new intensity. "I keep asking myself the same question," he confessed. "I know I've never given you the answers you need. I was selfish. What I did was a betrayal to you and to Ryan. I wish I had an excuse. I don't."

His green eyes, the ones she'd fallen in love with, hadn't changed, but she had. "I've been thinking about divorce," she admitted.

The thought had cropped up in her mind more and more. It would devastate Ryan and Kate admitted to herself, she would have a rough time emotionally too. Marriage was forever and she didn't care what the national average for divorce was. It's how she'd always viewed her love for Sam.

He stared at her, eyes intense beneath his furrowed brow, the foot over his opposite knee jumping to some unknown rhythm in his head. She couldn't quite decipher his expression as he stared past her shoulder.

His attention came back to her and now she could read the guilt he carried. "If that's your decision, I won't contest it," he said with resolve.

His major concern since the accident had been her well-being. Maybe he'd finally realized she would survive without him. Right now she hated him. Sam was too accommodating, and guilt made him so. Would he still be here if not for the accident? She had her doubts. Could she love him the same way again? Her emotions on that score were a rollercoaster. She finally understood why hate and love were similar emotions. Both carried too much baggage.

"I won't pressure you," he assured her. "If you want to go straight to your dad's, we can do that." He ran his hand through his hair. "I thought this trip was to give us space and possibly move forward—" he trailed off.

Guilt-ridden, Sam again. He played the part so well.

"For me, divorce is moving forward," she declared, her hands shaking. She shifted them to her lap so he couldn't see.

"I love you," he said. "I hurt you. If there was anything I could do to take it back, I would. I won't contest a divorce if that's your final decision."

"I need more time," she told him. She'd said this again and again because she wasn't sure what else to say.

She finished her wine and wheeled herself to the stairway, rode the lift down, and transferred to her other wheelchair. It was too early to go straight to sleep, and it irritated her. She reached for her cell. With one bar, she called her father, seeking comfort in his voice.

"Hey, pops," she said with a touch of excitement she didn't feel but her father would expect. "We had a great white spy-hopping on us today."

"Interesting. How big?" he asked thoughtfully, lacking the excitement she expected.

"I would guess at least the fifteen-foot range. I only saw the upper part of its body. It was a large one."

"Did Ryan see it?"

"Yeah, and you'll be getting a full retelling along with her daily log."

"That's my girl," he said with pride and then added, "I don't want to make you nervous, but we had two teens disappear from a small fishing boat about three miles from the lab. They only found pieces of the boat, but they've identified it as a great white attack. The bite circumference puts it at around eighteen feet. What's more unusual was they have a clear jaw pattern of two different sharks."

"Two?" Kate asked, slightly startled.

"They've been monitoring several shark pairs around the world. It seems to be males, and they don't always swim and hunt together, but they meet back up and continue traveling as a pair. Dr. Cordova is coming back early from South Africa to look at the boat and give us his opinion."

Interesting. The doctor was one of the top great white shark biologists in the world and her father had worked with him several times.

"You know the chances of us running into the same sharks are infinitesimal, right?" she asked. Her father's career studying stingrays paralleled with sharks, and she'd never known the larger creatures to make him nervous.

"What I know is one thing, what my gut tells me is another," he said. "It's possible one of the boys was bitten, and the other jumped in to save him, and they both drowned. That's what science wants me to believe. But that boat was demolished by sharks, which is very strange behavior. For decades we've destroyed their environment." He trailed off before he went into the dying ocean lecture that Kate expected. The state of the open seas was wreaking havoc with stingray habitats, and it drove him crazy that land lovers weren't paying attention. The demise of the oceans would be the demise of humanity. "I only want you to be aware of what happened here." His voice changed. "Seeing a great white spy-hopping is an amazing experience."

"The only thing that freaked me out was it didn't make a sound," she said honestly. "Not a splash, nothing. It could have disappeared below the surface, and we would have never known." She could not tell Sam this, but her father's fear was always a healthy one, and she trusted his years of experience around sharks.

"I told you about the one I came face to face with while chumming in the Gulf of Mexico," he said. "I'll never forget the shark's ability to do a spy-hop so silently. Freaky is probably a good word for it." He changed the subject as the crackle of his voice worsened with their phone connection. "How are you feeling?"

"Good. Your granddaughter thinks her primary job is monitoring my bowel movements, and I feel my job is to stay away from bad puns when she does it."

He laughed, as she knew he would. She gave him their current co-ordinates and their direction of travel.

"My next call might come on the radio. Cell service is spotty, and I got lucky tonight."

"Gotcha. I love you," he said before they disconnected.

Kate leaned against the backrest of her chair, suddenly feeling too weary to go through her nighttime ritual. Sharks and faithless husbands had worn her out. Her father wasn't aware of Sam's infidelity, and she knew if and when he found out, it would devastate him. He loved Sam and treated him like a son.

Kate lay in bed, staring at the ceiling for over an hour before she fell into a restless sleep. A hand ran across her stomach, and she rolled toward Sam, only to find it was the extra pillow in her berth, and she had dreamt of the intimate touch. She squeezed the pillow to her, feeling totally lost.

Kate missed him so much. She missed their intimacy and their conversations long into the night. It sucked the most that Ryan was in the mix and had to be considered, in Kate's choice. Then she was angry Sam gave in so easily over the talk of divorce. If he truly loved her, he should fight for her.

Kate rolled to her other side and pulled the extra pillow over her head. It would be a long night.

DAY FOUR, MORNING

After waking up earlier than she wanted to, Kate discovered the yacht traveling at a greater speed than usual. It was easy to deduce that Sam was taking them farther away from the great white shark. They were now most likely outside the coordinates she'd given her father. She chose not to dwell on it as she readied herself for the morning.

Shuffling through her clothes, she decided on a loose pink tee and a pair of black shorts. She had another gauzy dress she could put on after her workout and shower. She wheeled herself to the bathroom and looked at her face in the mirror as she pulled back her hair. One day she would need makeup that she would never use. Everyone aged and, other than moisturizers for the skin she often abused with the sun's rays, she wouldn't give in to the "younger looking is better" model of aging. She had a touch of pink on her cheeks that made her appear healthier than she had over the past year and a half.

She'd mostly confined herself to the house and doctor visits since the accident. In the beginning, she was self-conscious about her legs and the things she hadn't learned to do for herself yet. Two trips for a few food items and the feelings of helplessness they brought on in a world that no longer conformed to her was enough to keep her home. Sam had tried to get her out of the house more and went so far as to look into local book groups. She resented his interference. When she had to go into public, she felt as if there was a large letter painted on her forehead. Maybe a large C for my husband cheated. His infidelity embarrassed her, and she hadn't been honest with her tight-knit group of friends, which placed a wedge in her relationships.

Kate had always been the one with the ideal marriage, a daughter who was smart beyond her years, and a job she excelled at. That was all gone now, and she was really sick of feeling sorry for herself. When their voyage ended, she would look up her friends and reconnect again. They had tried to be there after the accident, but Kate pushed them away because she couldn't share the problems in her marriage. Pride had been her downfall, and she was sick of it getting in the way.

Sam cheated. He wasn't the first married man to do it, and he wouldn't be the last. She had to find the strength to figure out the next step in their relationship. Once she did, she would stick to her decision and build her life back, with or without Sam. That decided, she wheeled out of the room. The scent of bacon greeted her as soon as the cabin door closed behind her. Sam had been busy.

"Good morning," he said when she approached.

Today he wore tan shorts and an olive, short sleeved, cotton shirt with the buttons undone. She hadn't realized he'd bought so many yacht clothes. Sam appeared relaxed and she resented the fact that he'd most likely had a good night's sleep.

"Mom!" Ryan yelled, running from the table and launching herself into her mother's arms.

Kate lifted her daughter into her lap and gave her a big hug, glancing over Ryan's head at Sam.

"She's been helping me cook," he said. "We had an accident with a carton of eggs, but other than that, it's been a success."

Ryan giggled against her chest.

"He made me clean them up, and they were gooey," she told her mom.

"The entire carton?" Kate asked.

"Goner," Sam confirmed.

"Good reason for a big hug," Kate said, squeezing her daughter extra hard.

"Mom, I can't breathe," Ryan wheezed theatrically.

"Promise you won't waste any more eggs," Kate said cheerfully.

"Promise." Ryan squirmed out of her arms and went back to the table.

"I tried to call Grandpop this morning," Ryan told her. "We don't have internet."

"I called him last night and he knows communication might be a problem for a few days."

"You told him about the shark, didn't you?" Ryan accused, her eyes squinting with disgruntlement.

"Yes, I mentioned it, but he'll enjoy you telling him just as much."

Ryan stuck her tongue out before her nose went into her iPad.

Sam placed a mug of coffee in front of Kate. Just the smell perked her up a bit.

"Thank you," she said before taking a sip. Every coffee meme was written for her. She'd been drinking it since she was Ryan's age but wouldn't tell her daughter that. Mornings needed coffee like sharks needed teeth. Step between her and her cup and there would be trouble.

Bobbie, Kate's mother, had been an adventurer, just like Kate's father, and they both loved the ocean. Bobbie died of cancer when Kate was a toddler, and she had no memory of her. This gave Kate's father the opportunity to raise his daughter according to his tenets, and coffee was a huge one. He'd probably slipped Ryan caffeine without Kate being aware but she refused to think about it. Her father would just say it's what grandpops do and his behavior wouldn't change.

Sam's parents lived in upstate New York, and they weren't a close family. He called them on Christmas and their birthdays. It was the only time they spoke because they never reached out to him. They'd seen Ryan exactly twice, and that was because Kate and Sam went to them. Kate had received a get-well card after her accident and no other words of encouragement since. Not seeing Ryan grow up was their loss.

Kate grabbed a piece of bacon and ate it in two bites. "Not bad," she declared. "You can take over galley duty if you'd like."

"Yuk," Ryan said dramatically. "Remember the spaghetti?"

"You will not mention the great spaghetti fiasco on this boat," Sam said sternly, giving her a light tap on the head with the spatula he held.

"The spaghetti was bad, Dad." Ryan smiled and clapped her hands. "That rhymed."

"It was as good as your hood," Sam said, giving her a small tickle at the waist.

"I didn't bring my hoodie on board, and hoodie does not rhyme with good. You're silly."

"You're a silly filly," he said straight-faced.

"If you keep going," Kate told them, "I'll eat all the bacon, and there will be none left which will leave you Makin' more bacon." She ate another piece.

Even her daughter groaned when Kate joined in their word game.

Breakfast was filled with rhymes and laughter. Kate's world had been divided into "before he cheated" and "after he cheated". It beat out "before the accident" and "after the accident". Sam had basically pulled the rug from beneath her feet, and she had to find a way to move forward. Her unsolved issues wouldn't keep her from laughing with her goofball daughter when she was in a silly mood.

"I need your help in my cabin," Kate told Ryan after the dishes were stowed and Sam had moved into the control room. "It's bathroom behavior, so you should be happy."

Ryan placed her hands on her hips and glared at her mother in mock fierceness.

"You're lucky to have me. If Dad was your only nurse, that would be embarrassing."

Ryan had completely missed the point of Kate's embarrassment, which she guessed was normal for a five-year-old. They went to Kate's berth where she pulled out the small case Ryan would need.

"Urine test first, and then you can take my temperature." Kate could do both herself, but it would hurt Ryan's feelings. She took her caregiver role seriously.

Ryan was waiting with gloves when Kate wheeled out of the bathroom and handed the urine over. Ryan set it carefully on a small table, took out a strip, and dipped it like a seasoned lab tech. She then used her waterproof watch to monitor the time. The test was twofold and checked nitrite levels at one minute and leukocytes at two. She matched both to the color strip on the side of the box when it was time. Urinary tract infections were dangerous for paraplegics, and Kate did the test once a week and took her temperature daily.

"Looking good, Mom. I just need to check your temperature." Ryan removed the gloves like a seasoned nurse and took the thermometer out of the case.

When the thermometer displayed a precise 97.6, Ryan's small hands diligently marked the information on the chart. Ryan looked so proud of herself when she finished, and Kate was proud of her too. She would need to get a video so she could show her future grandchildren if Ryan decided motherhood was the right path. Above everything, Kate wanted her daughter to be happy and have the freedom to make her own choices in life.

"I did so well on the tests, maybe I can get out of physical therapy this morning," she teased her daughter.

The same small hands went to her waist again, and she glared at her mom.

"You're just being lazy," she said.

"Spoil sport," Kate replied, and this time she stuck out her tongue. They headed for the deck.

"I was thinking of taking Ryan out on the Sea Doo," Sam said when her physical therapy was done. "If you're comfortable, you can swim, and we won't go far."

Ryan jumped up and down.

"Go grab your vest," Kate told her.

The Sea Doo was stored on the platform at the stern. Kate didn't mention the shark because she was glad Sam was going back in the ocean, even though he was cheating slightly by using the watercraft. Ryan came out with her purple, blue, and yellow vest, so Kate could help her get it on. Sam grabbed his plain black vest and snapped the connectors in place. Kate sat on the end of the platform, her legs in the water.

"I'll stay close to the boat," she told them. "Have fun."

"We'll keep you in sight," Sam said after he unhooked the bar that kept the Sea Doo in place. He started the motor. Ryan jumped behind him and wrapped her arms around his waist.

"Let's go," she shouted, and they took off.

Kate slipped into the water. It felt so good on her body after the workout. Clouds were building out at sea, and small waves were rocking the yacht. It was still warm. She took a lap around the boat, and of course, her thoughts were on the shark. Seaweed startled her when it brushed her arm and it was simply too much for her to take. She swam back to the platform and stared out at her husband and daughter. She saw a flash in the water from the corner of her eye and turned her head slightly to see if she caught it again.

Nothing.

She scanned the surface of the ocean. Her gaze followed the small undulating ripples that went on for as far as she could see. Each splash against the yacht seemingly whispered about something hiding beneath the water. Her body remained tense. She used her arms to lift herself onto the platform and then reached down and lifted first one leg and then the other leg. She turned her body sideways so her feet were no longer hanging over the side. She wrung her hands, a visible sign of her inner turmoil, her eyes scanning the horizon for the creature that haunted her imagination. Despite the beauty of the overcast day, her fear, though ridiculous, was real.

"Look at us, Mom," Ryan shouted.

The Sea Doo did a donut in the water before Sam took off at high speed and did his own trip around the yacht. Kate waved, and at the same time, she was mad at herself for allowing her imagination to have a field day.

She decided she was being ridiculous and she needed to get back in the water. She had just started to lift her leg when Sam pulled the Sea Doo up close.

"You didn't swim for long," he said. Both he and Ryan were wet from the donuts. Ryan's smile was huge and there was no way Kate would ruin her day.

"My side cramped," she lied. If Sam wasn't worried about big sharks, she wouldn't say anything to him either. She hadn't told him about the missing teens, and she had no plans to.

"Are you going out again?" she asked.

"No. Our daughter has challenged us to a Yahtzee tournament."

"Oh no, the dreaded Yahtzee." Kate shuddered dramatically. "I thought she'd beat us too many times to play against her again?" she teased.

"I trounced you," Ryan said with glee.

"You always trounce me," Kate complained. "But I guess. Maybe you'll let me win so my feelings aren't hurt."

"If I win, we get to watch *The Little Mermaid*," Ryan told them ignoring Kate's comment.

Both Kate and Sam groaned.

8

Day Four, Afternoon

"You wanted to watch the movie again, so you put it away," Kate told Ryan after they finished *The Little Mermaid* for the hundredth time, although that might be an understatement. Ryan had been enthralled with the latest version of the classic since Kate and Sam took her to see it.

Kate's father, Greg, taught Ryan to play Yahtzee at around three years old, and she rarely lost now. More than anything, she had luck on her side. Kate had never seen so many Yahtzees thrown by one person. They teased Ryan about being the Yahtzee princess and they suffered through her favorite movie when she won. This time Sam snuck off quietly and Ryan hadn't noticed.

Leaving her daughter to place the video back in its case, Kate wheeled herself out on deck and looked across the blue water. The ocean had settled, and everything appeared calm. Kate didn't understand why an uneasy feeling stayed with her. She thought about the two missing teens. People drowned on the water; it was one of the dangers the ocean posed. Great whites mouthed and nosed boats but they did not tear them apart. The attack on the boat made no sense unless the sharks were going after the kids, which really made no sense. Her father had sounded worried, which didn't alleviate Kate's fear either.

She glanced at her hands on the sides of her wheelchair. That was it. The old Kate had never been afraid of the water, even when large sharks were sighted. She'd been in shark cages and had also done free swimming with the giant creatures. The accident and the subsequent loss of the use of her legs left her skeptical about what she was capable of. Even if she hired help, could she take care of herself without Sam in her life? She refused to continue the marriage simply because she need-ed a caregiver. Their future together, if they stayed together, hinged on the potential for salvaging their relationship and the repercussions of Kate's choice, particularly considering its impact on Ryan.

Her thoughts drifted back to Sam's confession.

"It wasn't what you think," he said during one of their many argu-ments after his confession. "She meant nothing. I never made promises to her."

"Stop," Kate held her hand up and then placed it back down. She was too worried she would punch him. Slapping was simply too good for the stranger standing in front of her. "I don't want to know details, I just need to know why."

That's when Sam's face took on the blank expression that she would grow accustomed to whenever the conversation came up. At least his blank face was easier to bear than the guilty one.

"I swear she meant nothing," he repeated in anguish completely misunderstanding her agony.

Kate's shock ran too deep to even put her thoughts into words, but anger was setting in and she would give them a go.

"Why are you even telling me this? What does it say about you?" Her voice rose even more. "You, a married man, slept with a woman you didn't love. Was it to hurt me?" Kate used the back of her hand to wipe away her tears. "Do you hate me? Is that it?"

"I love you, I swear. I don't know why I did it, but it was entirely my fault."

She stepped closer, her finger almost touching his nose. "Hell yes it's your fault. I thought we had a good marriage." Air caught in her throat. "I thought you loved me."

"I do, I swear it."

"You did this to our family. You don't know the meaning of the word." She'd stormed down the hall and locked the bedroom door to the room they had shared since they'd bought the house. She hadn't slept that night. She'd cried and thought of ways to get back at the other woman. Not that she would, and the longer she thought about it, the more she realized it wasn't the woman's fault. It was Sam's. And maybe her own.

A solid thud vibrated slightly through Kate's chair and into her arms that were holding the sides. It came from beneath the boat and brought her out of the horrible memory of that fight. She wondered if Sam was below deck in the engine room. It was the only place she couldn't access with her wheelchair. She waited but heard nothing more. A few minutes later, Sam fired up the yacht's engine. After a brief grinding noise that wasn't normal, they jolted forward, sending Kate's wheelchair toward the gunwale. She took a firm grip on the rail and looked over her shoulder through the window and saw Sam, who stood at the control center. He gave the throttle another try, and the weird sound came again. He lifted his hands when he saw her watching.

She wheeled back inside and made her way past the galley to her husband.

"Shut it down and try again," she said when she saw him studying the programmable logic controller known as the PLC. It was the nerve center of the yacht and showed everything from fuel consumption and engine performance to water levels and available solar power.

Sam pointed to the temperature monitor and shut down the engine.

"It's a little high but still within norms," Kate said as she closely examined all the readings. The engine turned over, and Sam moved the throttle the slightest bit. They heard the sound again.

"We need to use the two-ways," Kate said, rolling toward the shelf where they charged when not in use. "Go down to the engine room and listen to the noise and see if you can identify it."

"You want me to turn the engine off again?" he asked when she handed him the walkie-talkie.

"I'll do it. Let me know when you get there, and I'll start it back up." Sam headed to the engine room while Kate waited. Ryan was in her bunk, most likely watching *The Little Mermaid* again.

The radio crackled. "Nothing obvious down here. Turn the engine over."

Kate pushed the button that started the motor, and it sounded normal. "Anything?" she asked.

"No. Try the throttle."

Kate pushed the button on the locking latch then pushed the throttle forward. The yacht gave the same jolt it had when she was on deck.

"Shut it down," Sam called through the two-way.

"The engine temperature went up another notch," she told him when he came back into the control room.

"I think we could be caught up on something," Sam said.

Kate had been thinking the same thing.

"I'll gear up on deck then take a look at the propellers." Sam walked out of the control room after she nodded.

Kate wheeled herself to the deck and watched as Sam opened a deck mounted cargo container and began unpacking the scuba gear. He'd gone through certification years ago at Greg's insistence. At the same time, Kate enrolled Ryan in a bubble training course for young divers, but her daughter thought it was stupid because they could only go a few feet below the surface. Her grandpops took her much further down and gave her proper credit for how seriously Ryan took scuba safety. Sadly, Kate had lied about Ryan's age to get her into the course because she had still been too young. Her child was far beyond most children when it came to anything ocean, and Kate should have saved the money.

"Don't forget a knife," Kate told Sam when he was ready. She turned her wheelchair slightly and refused to examine the water's surface. The worries she'd had were stupid, and tonight with wine, she would laugh at herself.

She wheeled over and rummaged in the container, pulling out a sheathed knife and placed it in his outstretched hand. He attached it to his waist strap and checked the tank gage. He placed the mouthpiece into his mouth after Kate followed him to the platform.

He removed it and looked at her. "Give me ten minutes," he said.

"Sounds good."

Sam fell back into the ocean, righted himself in the water, and swam beneath the boat.

Kate looked at her watch and mentally recorded the time.

"Where did Dad go?" Ryan asked within seconds of her father disappearing from sight.

"He's checking to see if something is caught in the propellers," Kate said.

"Damned fishermen," Ryan replied, the low grumble in her voice showing her anger.

"Ryan," Kate said sternly.

"I know, Mom, but Grandpops says it all the time."

"That doesn't mean you can repeat it," Kate chided. She needed to speak with her father about his language, which would get her absolutely nowhere.

Greg was a free spirited marine biologist. Kate had been raised with few rules other than those pertaining to water safety. His eyes still sparkled with the passion of his life's pursuit or at the fury over those destroying it. The approach to his work was unconventional and guided more by intuition and a heartfelt connection to marine life.

Maybe his whimsicality was why she wanted a more structured life for her daughter. The thing was, Kate was okay with just about anything her father said to Ryan and thankfully Sam felt the same way.

"They leave nets behind, and it kills the ocean," Ryan insisted with reddening cheeks and a pursed mouth that displayed true outrage.

"And that still doesn't mean you can use bad language," Kate said and checked her watch. He'd only been down for two minutes. Her bizarre imagination had to be put to rest.

"We've been hijacked by a ghost net," Ryan lamented in a sad wailing voice that made a small grin appear on her mother's lips.

"Your father will un-ghost us," Kate assured.

"If Dad brings the net up, I'm measuring it and adding it to my logbook," Ryan promised.

A small splash sounded as Sam reached the surface. He spit out his mouthpiece and grabbed the platform with one hand.

"Damnedest thing," he said. "There was a large shark caught in a driftnet, and that was caught in one of the propellers. I think it was your sky-hopping shark."

"Could you save it?" Kate asked, her worry about the large shark gone and her concern over it at the forefront.

"Too late," he said. "I cut the net trying to get it untangled from the gear shaft. I need to go back down to finish the job, but I wanted you to know that I found the problem." He placed his mouthpiece back in.

"Poor shar—." Kate didn't have a chance to finish her statement when Sam's body was hit from below.

He rose up, his chest high above the surface. His body jerked and then was pulled several feet from the boat before he went completely under.

Kate watched in horror as blood filled the water.

9

Day Four, Afternoon

Kate sat frozen, completely paralyzed by what she'd just witnessed. Her cry faded into a sharp keening noise with no realization she was making it. The attack happened so fast that she momentarily wondered if it was her imagination. Her eyes scanned the water. No Sam. Then, like a bullet, his head shot above the surface, his expression startled, completely unaware of what had happened.

But Kate knew.

"Ryan, get the boat hook!" she yelled to her daughter, coming out of her trance, not taking her eyes away from Sam.

"Mom!" Ryan screamed.

Kate spun in her chair toward her daughter, but Ryan was looking in horror at Sam. No, it wasn't Sam who caused the reaction, Kate realized when she turned back. An enormous shark fin cut through the water a few yards behind Sam. The creature turned and swam closer, allowing Kate to see the massive jaws with multiple rows of deadly teeth. It rolled slightly and bumped Sam with its snout. Sam's body moved another foot from the boat. The shark slowly made another pass before it sank beneath the surface.

"Grab the boat hook!" Kate yelled again. She slid off her chair onto the swim platform and inched her body toward the water.

"Don't," Sam called, his eyes now wide with understanding and resolve.

"Move as little as possible," she told him calmly even though she felt the exact opposite. Ryan slid the boat hook beside her, and she grabbed it. "Grab hold of my shorts at the back and hold me as tight as you can," she instructed her daughter. The boat hook was retractable, and she pushed down on the lever and pulled on it until it was a foot longer. "Sam, grab this," she said, thrusting the hook toward him.

He didn't reach for it as he gently waded in the water, his body barely moving. "Sam, you must grab hold." He still didn't move, so she moved closer to him.

"Mom don't go in," Ryan whimpered, her green eyes the size of saucers.

Kate ignored her panic. "Keep holding tightly to my shorts, but don't get on the platform," she said. The shark could attack again any second. Great whites enjoyed befuddling their prey with a solid hit. When their target was close to death and had given up the fight, they usually followed up with a bite that had four thousand pounds of jaw pressure behind it. She had to get Sam out of the water.

She thrust the pole toward her husband and turned it in her hands so the hook got him beneath the armpit. She pulled with everything she had and heard Ryan's deep grunt as she held onto Kate's shorts. Sam's body hit the hull.

"Help me get you out of the water," she yelled at Sam. His hands reached for the platform. She grabbed him around the shoulders and tried to roll away to bring him out, using every bit of her upper body strength. Ryan could no longer hold onto her shorts and let go after a small grunt.

"Help me, Sam, please," she begged. "I won't let go of you."

He finally understood and used what strength he had left to get onto the platform. At the same time, a horrible sound came from his mouth, a mix of pain, fear, and determination. Blood immediately covered the deck. They were still too close to the water. Kate moved back, pulling Sam with her. Each agonizing inch felt like a mile. She didn't look at Sam or the blood, she focused on the water. Her useless legs wouldn't help and she had to lean forward, pull him back with her arms, use her arms to pull herself back and start all over.

The shark came to the surface, its powerful body rising up, watching them, then lowering slowly until it sank from sight again. It was the incentive Kate needed to make the final pull that got Sam clear of danger.

"Move my chair," Kate told her daughter.

"Where?" Ryan asked, her voice raw with heavy tears.

"Closer to me," Kate replied.

Ryan situated the wheelchair, and Kate moved her legs so they dropped over the platform onto the deck side. She had to release Sam long enough to get herself into the chair. His glassy eyes didn't give her confidence that he wouldn't roll back into the water and if that happened, he didn't have a chance.

"Help pull me away from the platform," Kate told Ryan. "We need to get him inside the cabin. It will be easier if he's partially on the chair."

As Ryan struggled to pull the chair back, Kate grabbed Sam and used her arms to pull him against her chest. His legs made a thud when they hit the deck.

"Are you with me?" she asked, but he didn't answer. He'd lost too much blood, and she had to revise her plan.

"Ryan, go inside and grab the first aid kit. Bring it here and then grab all the clean towels from the cabinet."

Kate leaned down and used her hand to push against the side rail, allowing Sam's body to slowly spill onto the deck. She lifted herself from the wheelchair and dragged her body closer to Sam's legs.

A huge chunk of skin and meat had been torn from his thigh, exposing bone and muscle. Blood continued flowing, which made it the first priority. She grabbed the knife from his belt and slit the leg of his wetsuit, pulling it up on both sides until the cut flaps were above the wound. She tied them together as best she could but knew it wasn't tight enough.

Ryan's hands shook when she pushed the first aid kit toward her mom. "Is he dead?" she asked.

"No, and he's not going to die," Kate assured her, even though she didn't know if Sam could survive long enough for help to arrive. "You did good. I need to stop the bleeding," she said. "I've tied off his leg. He's going to need water to drink. Grab the towels and then go back for his water bottle."

Ryan stayed frozen, staring at the jagged shark bite where her father's leg was once whole. Sam's body convulsed for a few seconds before he went still again.

"Ryan, I need those things right now," Kate snapped. She hated to sound mean, but Ryan was in shock, and there was no time for it.

Ryan rushed from the deck with small whimpers of distress trailing behind her. The yacht gave a slight jolt, and somehow Kate knew it was the shark. Was this the shark caught in the net? Nothing made sense, and her thoughts were all over the place. She needed to slow her breathing and think.

Deep breath in, hold, deep breath out.

She pulled Sam's arm until she could grasp his wrist and check for a pulse. It was there. She looked at his leg again. So much blood had pooled in the wound and continued flowing onto the deck.

"Here," Ryan said.

Kate took the towels from her daughter. Ryan's green eyes were huge, puffy, and red from crying, but she was responding to what Kate said.

"Come here," she told her and lifted her arms. Ryan launched herself at her mother from a foot away and wrapped her arms tightly around her neck. She kept her head turned away from her father.

"You're doing great, and you're helping dad," Kate assured her, inhaling Ryan's scent to help calm herself. "I need to get a better tourniquet on his leg to stop the bleeding. I'm using his wetsuit right now, but I need something that's more effective. You did so good and the first aid kit will have something I can use. After I've slowed the bleeding, I'll go inside and radio for help. We're going to be okay," she insisted.

Ryan trembled against her chest and sniffed in deeply, not letting go.

"I need you to keep being strong," Kate told her.

"Is he going to die?" Ryan whispered.

"No, but we need to get him comfortable and call for a helicopter."

"Okay, can I help?" Ryan asked, then sniffed again. The words, though soft held the strength Kate needed from her.

Kate pushed Ryan back, kissed her temple, and gave her a quivering smile.

"For now, hold your dad's hand. Can you do that?"

"Can he hear us?" Ryan asked.

"Maybe. Talk to him and tell him he's safe."

Kate opened the first aid kit, knowing it was inadequate for what they needed. She went through the heavy plastic box and pulled out several items. The stretchy athletic wrap would need to do as a tourniquet and she unrolled it.

"I'm right here, Daddy. Mommy is going to save you."

Her daughter had more faith in Kate's abilities than Kate had, but the words still caused her lips to tip upward.

"Ryan, run inside and get the wooden spoon from the drawer in the galley and bring his water bottle." Kate knew she needed to give one command at a time, but her words were as jumbled as her thoughts, and it was difficult.

Ryan thankfully came back with the spoon and the water.

"I'm going to untie the wetsuit where I knotted it," she said, speaking the words aloud to help her focus on what was needed. "Hold the spoon out to me until I have the ace bandage in place."

Kate took the water and placed it beside them. She carefully untied the wetsuit before she arranged the stretchy bandage beneath his leg so she could tie it. Blood gushed onto the deck and made her hands slippery. She took the spoon from Ryan and pushed it beneath the tied bandage. She then turned it, tightening the tourniquet until the blood flow slowed. Once that was done, she grabbed towels from the stack her daughter had brought and put pressure on the wound.

Sam groaned. The towel quickly soaked with blood.

"Daddy, I'm here," Ryan told him. She hadn't called him daddy in years.

"Take this," Kate said, handing her daughter the water. "See if he'll drink a little."

Ryan poured some water into her father's mouth.

Green eyes, just like his daughter's, opened.

DAY FOUR, AFTERNOON

Sam's eyes remained open while his gaze stayed unfocused. Kate didn't know if he was aware of what was happening or not.

"You're okay," she said. "You're out of the ocean and on the deck of Ryan's Gift.

He didn't respond.

"Stay with him while I radio for help," Kate told Ryan, trying to stay calm. She didn't need to tell her daughter to keep away from the rail; she doubted Ryan would ever return to the water. The horror in Ryan's eyes was something Kate would carry with her for a long time.

Kate scooted away from Sam, using her arms, which were at their limits and made the process more difficult. She grabbed the wheelchair and moved it so she could lift herself into it. This was one of the harder things she had learned in the rehabilitation center, but it was the most important. Once she was situated, she was able to wheel around Ryan and Sam to get inside. She rolled past the galley up the short ramp to the control center.

The entire console was dark, not a single light blinked.

"No way," she said aloud as she realized the significance of what she saw. She lifted the radio and hit the speaker button knowing what she would get.

Nothing.

"Crap," she growled and looked toward the galley. There were no lights there either. They had blown another fuse. She resisted the urge to cover her eyes and scream. If she started, she might not stop.

Deep breaths, she silently reminded herself. Slowly what she had to do came into focus. First, she would get Sam inside, where she could see him while she used the two-way to communicate with Ryan and talk her through changing the fuse. Kate hadn't thought about the accessibility of the engine room when they remodeled the yacht, and she cursed herself for it now. She wheeled back onto the deck.

With Ryan's help, they got Sam partially onto Kate's lap. He thankfully went in and out of consciousness and didn't seem aware of what was happening. Kate pulled on the wheels and Ryan pushed from behind. It was a long, exhausting process. When they were finally in the galley, Kate had to stop and take a break.

"Grab the cushions from the bench seat and place them on the floor," she told Ryan and waved her hand in the general direction of the table, too tired to move quite yet.

After Ryan situated them, Kate took a deep breath, ready to continue. She rolled as close to the cushions as she could manage and literally pushed Sam from her lap. She moved back a foot so she could go down to the floor. She then dragged and pushed, limb by limb, to get him fully on the make-shift bed. It cushioned him from his head to his butt with his legs hanging down slightly. It didn't look comfortable but it kept his injury lower than his heart by two inches.

An idea flashed into Kate's mind. "Go to the lower deck and grab some pillows," she told Ryan. "We need to get his chest upright." Blood circulation and keeping his injury below his heart were something she had read about in the past.

Ryan returned with the pillows and they began the arduous task of dragging him higher up the cushions. Once they had him propped up slightly, Kate sat on the floor beside him, breathing heavily, and smoothed his hair from his face.

His eyes blinked open, his expression strained.

"Are you with me?" she asked.

"It was a shark," he mumbled.

"Was it the shark in the net?" Kate asked.

For several long minutes, he didn't speak. Kate had about given up when he answered, "No, the one in the net died. I never saw the one that attacked—" A seizure stopped his next words. His entire body shook, and his eyes rolled back in their sockets.

Kate held onto him, murmuring softly until the tremors stopped. When they did, his eyes closed and his breathing settled.

"I need to check the tourniquet," she told him although she didn't know if he could hear her. There was blood on the floor, and she would swear they left a gallon behind on the deck. The cushion was now soaked and his biggest enemy was blood loss.

Sam whispered something, but she couldn't understand.

"Ryan, please get my backpack from my berth. It's inside the closet." Once she had the pill bottle open, she took out two pills and placed her hand towards her daughter.

"If he opens his eyes, make him take these," Kate said.

She replaced the bloody towel with a dry one. There was a lot of blood in the open wound, and it soaked through the towel too quickly. She lifted it and saw jagged skin, blood vessels, strips of muscle, and bone. He would most likely lose the leg.

No, she wouldn't think those things. Keeping him alive was the important issue.

She'd read that a tourniquet could stay in place for several hours without harming a limb. It was all she could remember.

"Take these, Daddy. Drink the water. A little bit more," Ryan cajoled her father.

Kate waited for him to get the pills down. When his neck relaxed, she twisted the spoon a half turn. Sam moaned but didn't open his eyes. She pulled her cell phone from her backpack and checked for a signal. Nothing. She sent a text to her father just in case it could go through. A failure icon immediately popped up on the screen. She would try again later.

"Okay, Ryan baby, we need to talk," she told her daughter. "You did a great job getting your dad to take the pills." Kate hugged her then leaned away. "We blew another fuse, and I can't get into the engine room with my chair." Kate handed over her cell and realized her hands were still shaking. "I need you to go down there and take pictures for me. Can you do that?"

Ryan nodded, her large innocent eyes filled with distress and glistening with unshed tears. Kate had no idea if Ryan understood the danger her father was in.

"Once I have the pictures," Kate continued, "I can tell you how to put in a new fuse."

Ryan slowly absorbed what Kate was saying and she looked toward the hallway that held the short flight of stairs that went to the berths. Ryan knew where the lower hatch was located and Kate waited patiently for her to figure it out.

"Okay, Mommy."

Kate wanted to hug her again, but they needed help as soon as possible. Ryan's legs wobbled slightly as she left the galley with the phone in hand, looking entirely too young.

Kate checked Sam's pulse, internally cursing because they had no internet and she couldn't look up how to care for him. His heart rate was slow when she compared it with her own. Sam's pale face looked like a death mask, which made everything worse.

Ryan finally came back and handed Kate the cell. She looked through the images, processing what she was seeing. A picture was nothing like seeing it with her own two eyes but she had to make do.

"Good job," she whispered as she went through the photos again in frustration that she didn't want Ryan to feel from her.

Sam groaned and opened his eyes a small bit. They remained unfocused. Kate needed him on a higher surface, but his weight was beyond what she could lift.

"Give me his hand," Kate told Ryan, who had moved between her mother and father.

Ryan lifted his hand and Kate took it. She gently squeezed his fingers as she leaned over to reach him.

"I need your help," she said and waited. His eyes seemed to focus slightly. "We've blown another fuse," she continued. "The radio won't work." His eyes remained open, which gave her hope. "Ryan took pictures of the engine room, but I'm still not sure where the fuse is located."

She handed the phone to Ryan. "Move up to his head so you can show him the images."

Ryan shuffled over and went to her knees. She scrolled the phone so he could see the individual pictures. After about a minute, Sam closed his eyes.

"We can wait until the pills take effect," Kate said, hiding her exasperation at her own inability to do more.

"No," he whispered, the sound ragged. "I don't know if she can do it."

"She will if you show me where the fuse is," Kate promised.

His eyes opened again and he studied the last photo. "This is the inverter," he said and showed Ryan where it was in the image. He closed his eyes and leaned his head back.

Kate had Ryan grab the toolbox from below the seat where they'd removed the cushions. When Ryan handed it to her, she went through it and found several different fuses.

"Put these in your pocket," Kate said. "I don't know which is the right one, but it will match the one you remove. It goes in exactly like you take it out so pay attention when you remove it, okay?"

"I'm scared, Mommy. It's dark down there."

Of course it was. Thank goodness Kate had the flash on for the earlier photos. She felt like an idiot for not thinking about the darkness and how terrifying it had to be in these circumstances.

"I know you're scared," she said even though her heart broke for what she was asking. "You've helped so much and I know you can do this. Grandpops will be so proud of you when you tell him how much you helped your father." Kate removed a flashlight from the toolbox and handed it to Ryan. Looking into her child's eyes, Kate saw the frightened little girl. Ryan's lower lip trembled to hold back tears. She was being asked to do more than any child should ever be asked.

"Okay, I'm ready, Mommy," Ryan replied shakily.

Kate smiled in relief and squeezed her hand.

"Grab the two-way radios, and you'll take one with you. I'll be right here. If you get too scared, tell me, and I'll go to the hatch opening and wait for you." She didn't want to leave Sam but it might be the only way this would work.

Ryan looked from her mom to her father and Kate knew she understood. Ryan walked to the handhelds and handed one to her mother. Kate studied the image of the inverter on the phone again.

"This is what you're looking for," she said and enlarged the image. "This area right here on the box lifts up, and that's where the fuse goes."

Sam's eyes were still shut, and she hoped she gave the correct location. If not, they would adjust. Armed with the flashlight, radio, and fuses, Ryan, looking heartbroken, trudged back to the engine room.

Kate checked Sam's pulse again. He didn't stir.

Something hit the yacht with a thump. Kate's entire body jumped.

What the heck was the shark up to? Was it angry that Kate took its meal? The yacht was too large for a shark to take down. Eventually, it would give up and move on. Maybe the dead shark attracted it. Sam said he cut it loose, so its first easy meal and then its second were taken away. Her thoughts flashed to the teenagers who disappeared and had their boat destroyed by two sharks, but she immediately cut it off. Sam and Ryan were what was important.

Once they had the power restored, help would come.

Her gaze went to Sam. His deathly pale skin worried her. Heck, the two-ton animal beneath the yacht terrified her.

The radio crackled, and Ryan's voice came through.

"Mom, I took it out and put a new one in," she said.

Kate was so proud.

"Okay, you need to hit the second button on the right."

"This one?"

Kate smiled. "I can't see it, sweetie. There's a digital display on the box where you changed the fuse, and it's the buttons below it. The second one on the right. If it works, the panel will light up." Kate had seen the buttons in the phone image and had barely made out the on switch. It had to be it.

A few seconds later, Ryan's disgruntled voice came through the radio.

"It didn't work, and it smells bad in here."

"What kind of bad smell?" Kate asked.

"Like something burned."

Great. Kate didn't think things could get worse, but she was wrong.

DAY FIVE EVENING, DAY SIX MORNING

Kate had Ryan gather pillows and blankets from the berths. They set them up on additional cushions removed from the galley seats so they could sleep together. Sam's pain had heightened and she'd given him another pill. Thankfully, the narcotics were helping and he'd fallen back asleep.

The makeshift tourniquet posed a dilemma, but Kate decided his chances of keeping the leg were slim and it was his life she was more worried about. Bottom line, if she took the tourniquet off, he would quickly die from blood loss. She'd gone through the first aid kit looking for anything that might help. It held suture supplies, but there wasn't enough skin to bring the two sides together and sew and with the extent of the damage it probably wasn't a viable option anyway.

Kate wracked her brain over things she'd read. Thoughts of gangrene, blood poisoning, and massive infection ran through her head until she thought she'd go crazy.

Settling Ryan so she would sleep proved easier than it was for Kate to shut her brain down. Each time she closed her eyes during the night, the jaws of a giant shark tried to eat Ryan or Sam and it startled her awake. The bumps against the hull didn't help and they were getting on her nerves and heightening her anxiety.

In her childhood, Kate had interacted with many ocean animals, knowing they had different personalities and were smarter than most gave them credit for. This shark was sticking around longer than she thought it would. Was it too old to hunt? Was it injured? She knew more about sharks than the average person because of her father's research but nothing she remembered helped her figure out what the shark's goal was.

Sam drifted in and out of consciousness. Ryan slept through the night, her young mind overwhelmed and exhausted. They were both asleep when the first rays of sunlight shone into the cabin. Kate finally decided sleep wasn't happening and checked her phone. Still no signal. She sent another text and received the same failure message.

She needed to use the bathroom. That's when she remembered the electric water pump wasn't working either.

They could use buckets of sea water in the toilets so they could flush. Kate would eventually need to send Ryan back to the engine room to switch over the grey water tank valve so it would empty into the ocean.

They had a gallon container of water in the galley that would provide drinking water.

Her thoughts turned to other problems such as cooking. They had an emergency supply of sterno fuel cans. It wasn't the greatest solution but she was glad they had them. With water and food taken care of, she switched mental gears to their rescue.

Her father would notice something was wrong when he didn't hear from them. He might wait twenty-four hours before notifying the Coast Guard. Another yacht could see them too. There was an emergency flag onboard and also a flare gun.

Survival was her focus. Kate was determined that Sam would survive until help came.

"Mom," Ryan called from outside Kate's berth.

"Come in, I'm changing into something comfortable," she replied, having slept in her swimsuit with a T-shirt. "Is your dad awake?" she asked when Ryan entered the room.

"No," Ryan shook her tousled head of hair and rubbed sleep from her eyes.

"Are you okay?"

Ryan's tiny shoulders went up and down in a small movement that said everything.

"I need morning hugs," Kate told her and Ryan eagerly ran to her mother. Her arms formed a cocoon of warmth around her daughter, the touch seeking to shield Ryan from the harsh reality of their predicament. Ryan nestled against her and Kate herself found solace in Ryan's familiar scent and steady heartbeat. They stayed that way for a long time.

"It's time to make breakfast," Kate said when Ryan finally pulled away. "We have a lot to do, but I need coffee before anything." Dammit, she thought silently, the coffee maker wouldn't work without electricity. She would make do with the Sterno cans for boiling water. Coffee was a priority this morning.

"You want a ride to the stairs?" Kate asked her.

Ryan eagerly climbed into her lap and Kate wheeled them to the chair lift. Her arms were still sore from the previous day but the ropes had turned into a lifesaver. Ryan scampered up first and then hand over hand, Kate made it to the top. She settled in her above deck wheelchair and they made their way to the galley.

Sam, wrapped in a blanket, continued sleeping. She had given him another pill an hour before she got up and he might be out for most of the morning.

"I'm going to need lots of help today," she whispered to Ryan.

"Okay. Do you need me to take care of Daddy?"

"Absolutely, but you're also my legs. We need to hoist the emergency flag, which is in one of the containers on deck. I'll let you pull the rope that raises the flag after we eat. We also need a bucket to fill with sea water so we can flush the toilets."

Ryan's eyes grew larger. "Don't put the bucket in the ocean or the shark will get you."

And why hadn't Kate thought of that? They were surrounded by water that she couldn't use. "Smart call and you're right. No ocean water. The bucket can be filled from the tank in the engine room. How does cereal with milk sound?" The fridge wasn't running, and the milk would go bad quickly. They would be eating the food from the refrigerator today, hoping for rescue before the sun went down.

"Can I have the good kind of cereal?" Ryan asked.

Kate had allowed her to choose one sugary brand for the trip. "Absolutely. At times like this, sugar is good for us, so I'll join you."

Ryan smiled as Kate got out the bowls and milk. She made Ryan's first, but before she poured milk into her own bowl, Sam groaned.

"You eat, and I'll check on your father," she said.

Kate wheeled herself over with his water bottle. They managed to get half of it down the evening before and he needed more to help replenish the blood he'd lost.

She placed the bottle on the floor, put one hand beside it, and braced her other on the opposite side of the chair in order to lift herself down. Her arm muscles silently moaned at the overuse. "Hi," she said when she saw Sam watching her. "How are you feeling?"

"Like a shark bit me," he replied but smiled gently. "How bad is my leg?"

"Bad and you have a tourniquet to stop the bleeding."

"That must be what hurts so much."

Kate handed him the water. "You lost a lot of blood and you need to drink this. I can get you another pain pill too if you need it."

The yacht gave a small jolt.

"What was that?" Sam asked.

Kate glanced at Ryan, whose face was scrunched up. She was also biting her lip in fear. She understood what was making the sound, though Kate hadn't told her.

"I think you have a secret admirer," Kate said lightly to Sam.

"What?" he asked, not understanding what she was illuding to.

"The shark. He's been bumping the yacht since his snack got away." She motioned her eyes toward their daughter, and Sam took the hint.

"I'm a yummy fellow," he said lightly. "Are you okay, Ryan?"

She left the table and leaned down to her dad. "Can I hug you?" she asked.

"My hugs usually cost money but there are a few free ones for smart little girls," he told her. Ryan leaned against her father, and he wrapped his arms around her.

Ryan's back trembled and then she said, "I'm scared, Daddy. I don't like sharks." She tightened her grip on her father and cried.

Sam looked over Ryan's shoulder at Kate. She gave him a sympathetic smile glad that he was awake enough to alleviate Ryan's fear and a little bit of her own.

"You had better not tell grandpops that," he said gently to Ryan after a few moments. "That shark was hungry, and I was in the wrong place at the wrong time. If I had seen it coming, I would have used my kung fu moves to stop him. The shark got lucky."

Ryan giggled and sniffed. She turned in the direction of her mother and she appeared calmer.

"Do you think you could eat something?" Kate asked Sam. "The fridge isn't working, and we need to eat what's inside before it goes bad."

Sam's expression changed. He realized what she was telling him. They were in trouble. "I don't think I can help with the food, but I would take a sports drink. I know we brought some."

"I know where they are, Daddy. I'll go get you one." Ryan disentangled herself and ran from the galley.

"How bad are we?" Sam asked as soon as she was out of hearing range.

"Our priority is getting you medical help. We have enough food and water to last a month even if we lose most of what's in the fridge."

"What about that damned shark?"

"It can't get to us, and as long as that's the case, I'm not thinking about it," she told him.

"What's the plan?"

Kate gave a small shrug. "We wait for my father to notify the coast-guard and for them to find us. It should be in the next twenty-four hours."

Ryan came back with an orange sports drink and handed it to her dad. He drank the entire bottle, which was good news as far as Kate was concerned.

"I'll take you up on that pill," he said. "I need to pee, and getting to the bathroom won't be easy."

"Will the plastic bottle in your hand work?" Kate asked. "You shouldn't move."

"Oh joy, I get to be part of the bathroom humor," he said and offered Kate a smile. He took her hand. "Thank you. I'm not sure how you got me out of the water, but you saved me."

Tears formed in her eyes. Yesterday she was thinking about divorce, and today, she was thinking she couldn't lose this man.

"I love you," she said simply, understanding that she had never stopped loving him and that had been why she'd dragged her feet for so long. "No shark was going to eat you."

He kissed the backs of her fingers before he rested against the pillow again.

"Ryan, can you grab the pain pills for me? I placed them in the top drawer by the sink."

Ryan jumped up and at the same time, the shark hit the boat harder than before.

12

Day Six, Afternoon

Watching Sam suffer was agonizing. He tried to hide the pain, but sometimes it was too much. Kate felt relief when the medication took effect and he slept. The realization struck that he went through these same challenges when caring for her after her accident. She'd genuinely hated him those first months. No matter what she did or said, he hadn't given up on her. Now it was her turn.

She made a mental list and put what she had to accomplish into motion. Drawing on lessons from her father, Kate knew a fight for survival on the open water was about the most treacherous danger you could face and there was no time to waste. First she located the emergency distress flag buried beneath some yachting equipment. She explained the process to Ryan as she clipped the flag to the cord of the flagpole.

"Your turn," she said when it was ready. Pull on this rope and it will go up.

Kate worried over Ryan's gloominess while they worked so Kate showed more excitement than she felt.

"Great job, girlie." The "girlie" comment usually received a rejoinder from Ryan but she didn't take the bait. Kate finally garnered a bit more enthusiasm when she showed Ryan how to use the flare gun.

"How many flares do we have?" Kate asked after she'd removed a twelve inch case from one of two sealed deck containers.

Ryan counted them and looked up at her mother. "Twelve."

"Okay, I'll go through safety and then let you fire the gun so you know exactly how to use it. We'll keep practicing but I don't want to waste flares needlessly so we'll just use the one for now."

Ryan paid close attention as Kate explained how to load the flare gun and the general principle for firing it.

"Hold it above your head, arm almost straight up, and squeeze the trigger," Kate instructed, adjusting Ryan's arm to a sixty-degree angle. "Now turn your head away so the heat doesn't bother your eyes. Go ahead and fire it so you know how it feels. Maybe we'll get lucky, and someone will see it."

Ryan followed the directions carefully, resulting in a loud pop as smoke and a bright flame shot upward. They repeated the steps with the gun empty multiple times so Ryan would remember what she'd learned.

"Could a flare kill the shark?" Ryan asked.

Kate wasn't sure if her daughter wanted the shark dead or wanted it simply to go away. She was raised to respect the ocean's wildlife and to never harm anything unless it was life or death.

"It would only make the shark mad," Kate said, trying to stay neutral. Truthfully, she thought it would be better if the flare could kill it.

Ryan went back to pointing and squeezing the trigger of the empty flare gun. Ryan was too inquisitive for her own good, and she loved learning, so this lesson helped keep her mind off her father.

Kate unfortunately could not let go of the series of events that brought them to this point. Each domino of horror knocked the next one down. The last coordinates her father had would make it harder to find them when every minute counted for Sam. Greg would eventually call the Coast Guard for help, but would it be in time? She would fire another flare when the sun went down if they weren't rescued by then.

Thud. It vibrated through her chair.

The shark's reasons were unclear, and Kate continued puzzling over why it would behave this way. The insistent knocks against the hull were psychological torture. Angrily, she wheeled to the port side and held onto the rail while looking across the surface of the water. The shark hit the yacht again which took her perspective from irritation to anger. The glassy blue water held no answers and the animal wasn't making an appearance.

"Are you looking for the shark?" Ryan asked.

"I am. I want to see how big it is," Kate replied.

"It's the biggest one out there," Ryan said, sounding wise beyond her years.

Kate chuckled because her daughter was most likely right. She would need to ask Sam about the size of the shark he found entangled in the net. They were miles from land, and big sharks preferred deeper water.

She'd seen the shark that bit him, but her focus wasn't on the size of its body. She knew it was large but wanted a better idea of how big it actually was. The scene in her head that woke her up through the night only included its massive jaws.

Like her dreams, the missing teens wouldn't leave her mind. Could this be the same shark? She replayed the attack on Sam again, returning to what he discovered in the net. Great whites ruled the ocean with killer whales and humans as its only enemies. Kate's father spoke out sharply about fin hunters and overfishing the seas. Over one hundred million sharks were killed each year, which was a hard number to contemplate. Many died simply so someone could eat fin soup and others died in safety barriers so people could enjoy a day on the beach. Most didn't understand the importance sharks and other marine animals played in the circle of life.

Kate had been raised by her father to never eat fish. Nets and hooks were destructive to ocean wildlife and fisherman had been tossing what they no longer needed overboard for centuries. She'd passed these lessons onto Ryan. Her daughter had never eaten an ocean product in her life. Sam was another story. He didn't eat fish at home, but he admitted he had no problem ordering it on business trips. This was difficult for Kate. Just as Ryan had said the day before, the ocean was dying and everyone had to help or the planet would ultimately die with it. From plastics to net and hook waste, the seas were under-maintained and overfished.

Kate had taken a different path from her father, but it didn't stop her from seeing the catastrophe facing the oceans in the near future. She looked up to Greg, but she'd realized in her teens that activism wasn't for her even though his work made her proud. Kate had known since Ryan was three years old that she would most likely take the same path as her grandpops. It was something in her complete fascination with everything he taught her. Though she loved her childhood, Kate couldn't remember feeling that enraptured when she was young. She had no doubt her daughter would do everything in her power to spearhead ocean rehabilitation and conservation. Ryan loved everything about the water and hung on to each word her grandpops said.

When the decision was made to buy and refurbish the yacht, Kate knew the water was where she herself was most comfortable, even after years away. If anything could give her the courage to determine her future, time at sea would do it.

This shark's persistence disturbed her. The water seemed peaceful but that made events even more ominous. Adding to her mounting anxiety, the shark hit the boat several times in rapid succession. After another visual sweep of the ocean's surface, she turned to Ryan.

"We need to check on your father." Kate had to get her mind off the shark.

Sam hadn't moved, and his skin seemed warmer than it had been. It was a hot day, which didn't help and caused additional worry. She had a full bottle of sports drink waiting for him when he woke up. She also planned to get some soup down him.

She checked him thoroughly. The foot on his injured leg was deep purple. She wished she knew more about blood circulation, but she didn't, and she again regretted that she couldn't check the internet. She let him sleep while she and Ryan took inventory of their supplies. It passed the time and kept Ryan busy.

"Do you think we'll be out here for a long time?" Ryan asked.

"No, but I'm doing exactly what your grandpop taught me. Prepare for the worst is his motto, and it's a good one."

Ryan nodded in complete understanding, and Kate was thankful for her daughter's maturity.

"Is the shark mad at us?" Ryan asked after a thud from below.

Kate wasn't sure how to answer. She didn't want to frighten Ryan more than necessary.

"I don't know what the shark is thinking," Kate said honestly. "Your grandpop has told you about shark mouthing and bumping, right?"

Sharks used their mouths and snouts to identify objects they weren't sure of. The problem with mouthing was their teeth were large with serrated edges that could cause a lot of damage even if the shark was simply curious. Bumping also had consequences because great whites had thousands of pounds behind the bump. It was, however, what a curious shark did. Kate didn't feel the one beneath their boat was curious, but other than that, she wasn't sure what was happening.

"Yes, grandpop taught me that. Is the shark just bumping us?" Ryan asked with interest.

"That's what I think it's doing."

"Can it bite a hole in the bottom of the boat?" Ryan asked next.

"It's highly unlikely," Kate told her. This difficult conversation was necessary to keep her daughter calm, but it was also giving Kate things to think about. At the top of her list was why the shark kept bumping the boat.

It made no sense and she couldn't shake the ridiculous feeling that something sinister was in play.

Day Six, Evening

S am ate only four spoonfuls of soup. On a positive note, he finished off the sports drink. His temperature rose another degree, which worried Kate. Sitting on the floor with him had its drawbacks, and she decided to somehow get him to his berth if they weren't rescued by the following day.

What posed the biggest problem was getting the wetsuit off him so he could be as comfortable as possible. She waited for the pain pill to take effect and then cut the suit away. He had his swim trunks beneath it and they were dry so it would work. With limited clothes it would be much easier for him to take care of personal needs.

Earlier, Kate had fished out the handheld solar lights that were stored in a drawer beneath Sam's berth. She'd recharged them by placing them next to the window. Now the galley was lit up, and the ominous feeling Kate had carried didn't seem as threatening.

"Do you want to sleep out here or in your own bed?" she asked Ryan about an hour after the sun went down.

Ryan's lower lip trembled and her face paled. Kate immediately regretted asking.

"I want to stay out here with Daddy," she said timidly, which wasn't like her at all.

Kate's heart ached. "No worries. Your dad likes having you close by."

"I do," Sam said gruffly, making them aware he was awake. "You're my helper, and it makes me feel safe when you're near."

Ryan gave Sam a long hug.

"It's time to send up a flare," Kate told her daughter. "Do you want to fire it?"

"Yay!" Ryan jumped up and headed for the deck.

"Making her feel safe was short-lived," Sam said with a weary smile.

"She rebounds constantly, and I'm grateful for it."

"Are you doing okay?" he asked. "The floor can't be comfortable," he continued before Kate replied.

"I hate to admit it, but I feel safer with all of us together."

Sam reached his hand up, and she took his warm fingers.

"You and Ryan come first, no matter what happens," he said determinedly.

"We're a team," Kate told him. "The three of us, not just me and Ryan, so stop talking stupid or I'll take your pee bottle away."

His hand squeezed hers more tightly, almost to the point of pain.

"Keep Ryan alive," he said with determination.

He shouldn't be talking this way. They would all be safe.

"I need to get on deck before Ryan gets impatient and fires the flare without me," Kate told him.

Sam released her, and she hurried outside, unwilling to be part of his defeatist talk. Things were difficult enough, and she refused to consider that they wouldn't survive. She reminded herself that Sam had suffered a severe injury with extreme blood loss or he wouldn't be talking this way. Help was coming.

Ryan waited with crossed arms and a tapping foot when Kate joined her on deck. Her indignant pose made Kate smile and took away her irritation. Kate removed the flare gun box from the container.

"What if you give me a lesson on firing the flair gun this time?" Kate asked.

"Can I still fire one?" Ryan replied, her expression dubious.

"Absolutely. If you tell me how to do it correctly, it lets me know you can be safe with the gun and if for some reason I couldn't come out here, you could do it by yourself."

Ryan smiled, good with the new game Kate invented. Her small nose scrunched up in concentration while she removed the gun and a flair.

"You push the barrel away from the hammer like this," Ryan said and showed Kate how it was done. "That way you can load the flair like this." She bit her lip as she inserted the flair into the barrel. "You snap it back in place like this."

Ryan was super smart but even Kate was impressed with how much she retained.

"Then you hold it at an angle and fire. Do you want to try?" Ryan asked.

"Nope, that was an excellent lesson and you have safety protocols down. Go ahead and fire."

Ryan proudly fired the flare. It went up and dropped back down, the light only shining for about five seconds but it was bright and hopefully would be seen. They stood on the deck for a long time, watching and waiting, but they neither saw nor heard anything that sounded like another boat in the distance.

"Tomorrow, you and I are taking showers," Kate told Ryan when she finally accepted that the flare hadn't been seen.

"I was hoping you would say that," Ryan said with a devious smile. "You stink." She pinched her nose to bring home the point.

"You took the words right out of my mouth." Kate grabbed her daughter, pulling her close, and tickled her for a few seconds, delighted over the innocent giggles that seemed untouched by recent events. She hugged her tightly. "I love you," she whispered.

Ryan tipped her head back, and Kate kissed her cheeks, chin, and forehead.

"I love you too, Mommy."

A thump from under the boat ended their cheery mood. The shark couldn't have picked a worse time to alert them that it was still around.

"I want to go inside," Ryan said after looking downward where the noise and slight vibration originated.

The shark's insistence on terrifying them was even creepier in the dark. Kate stared out across the nearly black ocean, and a slight quiver ran across her flesh. The only sound was the water lapping against the yacht.

"I agree, let's go inside," Kate said as her fear ramped up.

They returned to the galley, and she gave Sam Tylenol for his temperature. He couldn't get comfortable and his flushed face made him look as bad as he felt. It took an hour before his temperature dropped steadily and he slept.

"Come on," she told Ryan after she heard Sam snoring lightly. "Let's get your teeth and hair brushed. We can read a story after that." Kate wanted to keep everything as normal as possible.

They each took a solar light and went to the stairwell of the lower deck. Kate used the rope to swing herself into the waiting wheelchair, suppressing a groan. When she was settled, she looked upward, where her daughter waited.

"Can I try it, Mom?" Ryan asked.

"Of course, let me back up." Kate rolled a few feet away and watched as Ryan swung down the rope and landed on her feet like a pro.

It had taken only a short time for Ryan to acclimate to Kate's disability. To her, Mom was Mom. Kate's proficiency at swimming in the exercise pool at the gym helped Ryan see her mother could still do many things. The loss of Kate's legs was simply part of Ryan's childhood.

"That was fun. Can I climb up the rope when it's time?"

"Absolutely." Kate realized getting Sam to his berth came with additional logistics problems she hadn't considered. It might be beyond what they were capable of. She decided to take it one step at a time. For now, getting herself up and down was proving more difficult than she expected.

When she brushed her daughter's hair, she noticed Ryan's shark tooth necklace. Sharks were not Kate's favorite animal right now. It was ridiculous that the tooth bothered her like it was some type of omen.

The faucet water trickled when they brushed their teeth. There was a lot to do on tomorrow's list and Kate felt exhausted just thinking about it. After they finished Ryan's nighttime ritual, she was ready for her story.

Ryan scrambled up the rope to the upper deck. For Kate, it wasn't as easy and it took twice as long to get to the top as it had taken her earlier. Ryan had to adjust the waiting chair for her and Kate was damp with sweat when she finally sat down. Once they had the inverter repaired or replaced and they took the yacht out again, Kate would use the rope once per day so she was more proficient.

They settled in beside Sam, and she read Ryan one of her personal favorites, *Ramona Quimby, Age 8* by Beverly Cleary. Kate made it a quarter through the book when Ryan grew tired. Thankfully, the shark hadn't bumped the boat in the past hour, and Ryan was able to settle down and fall asleep.

Kate snuggled in beside her on the cushions and welcomed the steady hum of her daughter's breathing. Sam continued snoring, which was not a habit of his, but for now, it gave her comfort. Unfortunately, Kate and sleep weren't on the best of terms at the moment.

She lay awake and her thoughts went where they always did, her marriage. Kate's therapist insisted Kate was not responsible for her husband's infidelity. That didn't mean Kate always believed it, and now, she was rethinking quite a lot. She had returned to her job when Ryan was old enough to vocalize life in daycare. Kate found that her career didn't hold the same excitement it once had. She felt guilty for leaving Ryan in the hands of strangers and most of all, she missed her.

There had never been enough time during the evenings after work to accomplish everything. Sam helped when he could, but he often traveled for his job. Kate hated how tired she felt. She'd wondered how working women did it with multiple children. She had trouble with only her daughter, and Ryan was a great child.

On the intimate side, Kate was often too tired for sex. Sam took it in stride and she had never questioned it.

Why?

She understood when Ryan was a baby because they both got little sleep in the first year. But after that, Sam was as trapped in their lifestyle as Kate. They had only ever wanted one child. Maybe if they had talked about their feelings in the beginning, the chasm she hadn't noticed wouldn't have widened.

Their family became a team of three and Kate had allowed the new dynamic to take away from the intimate side of her marriage. This didn't dismiss Sam's fault for his actions, but for the first time, she didn't feel the fury she normally did when she thought of him cheating. He'd sworn it was only the one woman. Unsure of the why, she finally believed him. Maybe it was because the shark attack made Sam vulnerable. The usual guilt in his expression was gone now and that helped too.

Kate rolled to her other side, almost falling off the cushion to the floor when she did. She fluffed her pillow. Her body was weary, but her brain stayed on high alert. After her attempt at sleep failed, she hauled herself to the wheelchair and grabbed one of the solar lights. She wheeled outside and shined the light over the water.

The dark ocean still evoked a sense of mystery in her as she looked across the surface. Its vastness so immense, it created an otherworldly landscape of soft, comforting sounds. The ocean still held fascination with geological wonders it hid far beneath the surface, in a world where silence reigned and time stood still. A half-moon showed across the water for as far as she could see and she turned off the solar light. The yacht swayed to the rhythm of the tide. The shark was still out there. The heavy weight of menace pressing down on her proved it. She didn't go back inside, refusing to allow the cold-blooded demon to intimidate her.

The shark hit the yacht.

"You will not win," she promised.

DAY SEVEN, MORNING

U pon rising the following morning, bleary eyed after little sleep, Kate tried the radio again in an act of desperation. There were still no lights on the console, and she didn't care. When the radio gave no sound, she sent another text to her father and received the same previous result. Frustrated and worried, she had to remind herself that her father might just now be contacting the coastguard. Help would arrive today and Sam had to hold on.

The milk in the refrigerator was questionable for cereal, so Kate made pancakes. The sterno fuel's small can made it a slow process because it only heated half the pan. Sam wanted broth, so she heated a can of chicken noodles and strained the large pieces out. He ate little. He also fought her over drinking water but managed a few sips.

"My stomach doesn't feel well," he said gruffly. "I'll drink more later."

His temperature was up, and Kate gave him Tylenol. Should they move him? She had no idea what to do. When he woke up again, she would ask. The move would be painful, and they needed his help to do it.

Kate's biggest concern was the wound beneath the bandage. She had to check on it and change the bandage which was mostly dry. Getting it off would be uncomfortable but couldn't be helped.

She had always felt independent even after her marriage. As a child, her father expected the same things from her as he expected from an adult. She was usually up for the challenge. Right now, she felt helpless, which took her back to the first months following the accident. If she could handle that, she *would* handle this.

Kate gave a long internal sigh and tried to focus. She needed to get Ryan clean. With no water pump, showers were not an option. It would need to be a bath in a bucket of water. She could then move Ryan to the sink and wash her hair.

"What about you?" Ryan asked after Kate told her the plan and crinkled her nose with humor.

Kate gave a small tug on her hair. "Don't worry, I won't make you live with my smelly body. I'll scrub up while sitting in my chair and you can help me wash my hair once the rest of me is clean."

Ryan ran a theatrical hand across her brow in relief and giggled until Kate gave her the bad news. "We need water from the engine compartment."

Ryan went from silly to scared and Kate silently declared herself the worst mother on the planet for putting her child through this. Tears filled Ryan's eyes and Kate pulled her close.

"I know this is hard and you're scared. The definition of bravery is when you succeed at something that frightens you. I'll be right above you at the hatch. We'll work together and you won't be alone."

"Okay, Mommy," she said with a sniff.

Kate carried a solar light on her lap. She wheeled to the hatch leading down to the lower berths with Ryan behind her carrying the water bucket with a rope attached to the handle. Like the day before, Ryan went down first. Kate got off her wheelchair and handed Ryan the light and bucket. She then used the rope to lower herself to the waiting wheelchair.

They went to the engine compartment hatch and Kate shined the solar light downward. After a quick hug, Ryan went down the steps with Kate's reassuring voice following her. Ryan filled the bucket directly from the water tank and Kate raised the bucket using the rope which she'd tied to the handle. Once it was up, she placed the bucket in her lap and wheeled it to the bathroom where she poured it in the tub. It took time to haul the water this way, but they didn't have another option. Overall, the plan went smoothly and after a few rounds of filling the bucket, Ryan was no longer scared. When they finished hauling the water, Ryan came up the ladder and they went to the bathroom to use what they'd worked so hard for.

The day was going from warm to hot, and the cold water wasn't too bad. She had Ryan stand in the tub while Kate lathered her with soap before pouring the cold water over her.

"Is this how you had to take baths when you were little?" Ryan asked as she stood with goosebumps covering her skin.

Kate couldn't help a small chuckle. "I'm old but not quite that old. The year I was born was the first year AOL came online."

Ryan looked at her blankly.

"America Online, AOL." Her daughter's expression didn't change, and Kate realized she was the foolish one on this subject. "Never mind. Hot water came out of showers a hundred years before I was born."

This seemed to satisfy Ryan, but Kate realized her daughter, though mature for her age, was far too young to face the danger they were in. She had an entire life in front of her and she hadn't lived yet. These thoughts stayed with Kate while she rinsed the soap off her daughter.

They refilled the bucket when Ryan was dry. Ryan helped get a towel beneath her on the wheelchair's seat without Kate leaving it. It took some wiggling, but they got it accomplished with another round of giggling.

When both their bodies and hair were clean, Kate dressed herself and Ryan, wearing a thin bathrobe went to her berth for fresh clothes. It took ninety minutes to complete their bathing. Feeling clean made the day's mental gloominess fade a bit. Ryan put on her favorite pale green jumper that made her look too cute for words. She was growing up much too fast. Her front tooth was beginning to wiggle and Kate couldn't help wanting to see a toothless grin.

They checked on Sam and found him sleeping.

"Let's dry our hair on deck," Kate said after checking his forehead. The heat coming off him worried her.

They grabbed their water bottles and headed outside. Kate's gaze immediately traveled across the water's surface. Ryan had moved closer to the platform to fluff her hair.

"Mom," she cried and slowly backed away, her eyes glued to the shark.

It's huge jaws grabbed the wooden slats of the dive platform. Kate wheeled closer to see its size. She had trouble absorbing the raw power it took to move the yacht back and forth. The large body, a mottled pattern of gray and white, with scars from prior battles with who knew what, was intimidating in its ferocity.

The shark released the platform and swam around the yacht. Its torpedo-shaped form glided effortlessly in the blue water. The dorsal fin cut through the surface like a sharp blade. Kate rolled her chair closer to the side rail to watch it. The shark slowed when it was in front of her and cold, dark eyes peered soullessly into Kate's before it rolled slightly to its side and continued on. Intelligence had burned in its gaze. She rubbed her arms and continued following its movements.

Claspers on its lower belly, identified it as a male. Kate judged it to be seventeen feet long and its weight over a ton. The shark was more than three times Kate's five feet, five inch height. The gills undulated with the flow of water coming from its jaws that were incapable of closing all the way. Muscles ripple beneath its skin, propelling it forward until it turned and disappeared into the depths again.

Seconds later, it struck the bottom of the yacht with such force that Kate rolled backward. At the same time she watched as Ryan let out a horrific scream.

Kate lunged too late to keep Ryan from falling into the water.

DAY SEVEN, MORNING

Terror stole Kate's ability to scream. Everything inside her rebelled at what was happening. She pulled herself frantically along the rail to where Ryan had gone overboard. She saw Ryan, her wet hair covering her face, wildly looking at the water around her while her arms flailed. Kate's voice returned.

"Don't thrash," she yelled.

Ryan instantly went still, her eyes desperately seeking help from her mother, and slowly she sank below the surface. Her hair floated for about ten seconds. Kate grabbed the rail and half lifted herself from the wheelchair, the adrenaline rush giving her strength.

Ryan had disappeared entirely and the water remained still. Kate frantically positioned herself on the rail so she could jump. A small splash came from the stern of the yacht at the platform the shark had just mauled. Ryan, soaking wet, scrambled onboard. At the same time, large jaws pitched from the water and closed ferociously around nothing but air, missing Ryan's feet by inches. It sank below the surface. Ryan scrambled away from the edge and launched herself toward Kate who had crawled back in her chair.

"I, I," Ryan said through chattering teeth. "It didn't catch me."

Kate had trouble believing Ryan was safe in her arms. The sight of the shark grabbing at her would stay with Kate for the rest of her life.

The underside of the yacht took a heavy hit from the shark again.

"Will it sink our boat?" Ryan whispered, holding onto her mother for dear life.

"No, I won't let it," Kate promised and realized for the first time that the shark wouldn't give up. It could have easily gone searching for food in another more plentiful area. The shark's mission was to take out the yacht. The only solution Kate had was to kill the shark.

The "how" was the problem. Holding Ryan, her thoughts became clear and she began putting together a plan. They had spearfishing gear left by the previous yacht's owner. They were in the larger of the two deck storage bins.

Before she tackled the spearguns, she gently pushed Ryan's wet body from her lap so she was standing on deck. Kate examined her from head to foot to ensure she was in one piece.

"I'm okay, Mommy," Ryan said, the trembling in her voice almost gone.

"I love you. Don't scare me like that again." Kate placed her arms out. "I need your help," Kate said after giving her another long hug.

With Ryan back on her lap, Kate wheeled to the safety lines attached to the deck. She circled one around Ryan's waist and clipped it. She then attached one to her wheelchair.

"This will keep us from falling in the water," she told Ryan while she worked. "When we're on deck, we need to stay safe. Understood?"

Ryan's small chin moved up and down as her gaze traveled to the ocean, her fear still evident.

What if she hadn't made it? The thought added to Kate's determination that she would find a way to stop the shark. She wheeled to the largest container. It stood beside the one with the diving equipment. Both containers were held in place by a metal rack. She unlatched and lifted the watertight lid. Inside, she found large hooks and braided line used for deep-sea fishing. It also held a nylon bag with a net. She handed the items to Ryan while she searched deeper inside. The spearfishing gear was at the very bottom.

There were two spearguns, which Kate examined closely. One was marked 90 centimeters, and the other 120. There were assorted spears and blue rubber tubing. Unfortunately, there were no directions. Kate had never used a speargun, but she would figure it out.

"Are you going to shoot the shark?" Ryan asked.

"Maybe. It's a backup plan, and it makes us safer if we're prepared."

"You sound just like Grandpops."

"He taught me everything I know," Kate replied with a smile, still in disbelief that Ryan had survived. "Let's check on your dad before we figure this out."

Sam continued sleeping. His face was unnaturally flushed, so Kate checked his forehead. He was burning up, even after the Tylenol had had plenty of time to work.

"We need another bucket of water," she told Ryan.

They hauled the water to the galley, and Ryan wiped her father's head and face with a washcloth while Kate tackled his arms, chest, and good leg. He mumbled but didn't wake up.

"Sam," she said at one point. He barely opened his eyes. "Drink," she told him.

"Don't feel good," he mumbled.

"Do you need a pain pill?" she asked.

He didn't respond, and his eyes closed. When she washed his good leg, she didn't like the smell coming from the injured one. Could the infection travel with a tourniquet on? She felt overwhelmed by what she didn't know. Would she need to amputate his leg? Could she if it was his only hope?

Again, she wanted to scream. Ryan held her together. She refused to let her daughter see her fear. She coaxed Sam awake and added another Tylenol to the two she had given him earlier. She wouldn't be able to give him more for six hours. Sam managed to swallow the pill and take two sips of sports drink before he fell asleep again. He hadn't taken a pain pill and she had no idea how long his rest would last.

"Let's figure out how the spearguns work," Kate said, to take her mind off Sam. If she wasn't being proactive, she would go insane.

DAY SEVEN, AFTERNOON

Kate and Ryan spent an hour working with the spearguns. They were too large for Ryan, but she assisted Kate in attaching the spear and figuring out how the rubber tubes worked and made the spear eject.

"These are dangerous," she explained. "I'll place them back into storage and move the other items to the scuba container so I can get to the spearguns quickly." Ryan was inquisitive but she understood when something was unsafe and would leave it be.

"Is help coming?" Ryan asked.

"Your grandpop is working on rescuing us," Kate said. "He had our last location, but we moved away from there. It will take time to find us, but he will, I promise."

"Is Daddy getting sicker?"

"He is, and I'm more worried about him than the shark. Maybe you can get him to sip more of the sports drink."

"I'll bribe him with kisses," Ryan promised.

"It's a deal. Let's go check on him and eat some lunch."

They found Sam talking incoherently with labored breathing. Dark circles beneath his eyes made him appear gaunt even with his flushed skin from the high fever. His upper body was half off the makeshift mattress, with the blanket thrown aside. 'Shark' was the only word Kate understood.

"We need to get him situated again and bring his temperature down," she calmly explained to Ryan, keeping the fear from her voice which wasn't easy. "If you want a snack, you can have one. It may be a bit before I prepare lunch."

"I'm good," her daughter said.

After rearranging Sam back on his makeshift pallet, they brought up another half bucket of water to cool him down. When she finished, Kate left a wet towel on his chest and one on the back of his neck. He still felt warm, but he'd stopped moving around as much, which was a good sign.

Kate was doing everything she could and she knew it wasn't enough. Sam was in serious trouble and the loss of his leg was no longer a factor. This was about his survival and she was fighting on many different levels. Her inadequacies didn't help and all she could do was move forward.

Lunch consisted of peanut butter and jelly. Kate removed the crust from Ryan's sandwich and cut it into a triangle the way she preferred it. Her daughter was convinced they tasted better this way. Kate ate hers with globs of peanut butter, a small amount of jelly, and an oblong cut. She placed chips on the table, and they drew straight from the bag.

Kate was exhausted. She hadn't slept the previous night and dropping face first into her food was a very real possibility.

"Do you think your old mom could take a nap?" she asked Ryan after they cleaned up and stowed the dishes.

"You're not old," Ryan chided. "I'll listen for the shark and let you know if he hurts the boat." Ryan was as serious as a doctor preparing for major surgery.

"Grab your coloring books," Kate told her. "You can sit at the table or down on the floor while I sleep."

"Go to bed," her five-going-on-fifteen-year-old told her. "I'll stay with Dad."

This was a lot for her daughter, but Kate could barely see straight. An hour of sleep in her bed would be wonderful. She thought about setting the alarm on her cell, but she was starting to worry about the inability to recharge so decided to shut it down.

"Don't let me sleep too long," she said. "If your dad wakes up, come and get me."

"I'll sit with him, color my pictures, and listen for the shark."

Kate wheeled over and kissed Ryan's cheek, the light touch giving Kate comfort. "I don't know what I would do without you."

Ryan smiled and began flipping through pages of a coloring book to decide what to work on. Kate surprisingly fell asleep as soon as her head hit the pillow. She woke up after the sun went down. There was a solar light next to her, and when she groped her way to the upper deck, she heard her daughter talking.

"He found the red hat under the tree."

When Kate entered the galley, Ryan was reading a book to her father. His eyes were open, and his skin didn't appear as flushed.

"It's dinner time," Kate said. "I slept longer than I expected."

Ryan jumped up and gave her a hug.

"I've been reading to Daddy. Some of the words are too big, and he said I could make them up."

"She uses 'poop' a lot," said Sam, a smile in his voice.

Kate gave Ryan a stern look and then laughed. "You and your poop humor." Her daughter just grinned. She turned back to Sam. "How are you feeling?"

"The pain is a bit worse, but my stomach has settled."

"Unfortunately, the pain pills could be the cause of the stomachache. Do you still want one?"

"I think I do. My leg feels like it's in boiling water, and it's getting worse. The bandage should be changed."

"It's going to hurt," she told him.

"I'll let the pain pill take effect before you get started and maybe add some wine."

"Do you feel like food?"

"Broth only, but I'm thirsty for water. Ryan forced me to finish an entire bottle of sports drink."

"Broth and water coming up," Kate said and gave Ryan a high five for making Sam drink the fluid.

He ate less soup than she wanted, but he drank more water than she thought he would. Kate felt better after the nap and she felt encouraged by Sam's change too, though she was not looking forward to removing the bandage. She boiled water using the smallest pot they had on board and added it to the colder water in the bucket so it was warm.

When her preparations were finished, she told Sam it was time for the wine.

"My stomach can't handle it. You have a glass," he told her. "You'll need it as much as I needed the pain pill."

Kate didn't argue and drank a large glass before she got started.

"It needs to soak a bit first," she told him when she was ready.

"Whatever you feel is best." With Ryan's help collecting towels, it was time.

Kate had used the last ace bandage to wrap around the towel covering the wound. She unwound it and poured water slowly onto the bloody towel that remained.

Sam hissed but managed not to cry out. Kate remembered the times after her accident when she couldn't act like a baby because of Ryan. She wasn't sure if that was good or bad because sometimes she thought screaming would have been better.

She massaged Sam's neck and shoulders until she was ready to remove the towel. "Does this feel okay," she asked.

"It feels too good." He groaned and circled his neck when she switched to his shoulders.

"I think your leg has soaked long enough. Are you ready?" She squeezed his fingers.

"Get it over with."

"You're sure?"

"It's got to be done."

Kate didn't have his confidence. She was afraid to see the damage, especially if there was the infection.

"I have peroxide, but it will hurt," she said. "Once we have the towel off, I can pour it on if you think you can handle it."

"I'll handle it," he said.

When he saw his leg, he would know the outcome, no matter what she did. The towel came off easier than she expected. She peeled it back and examined the torn flesh and mangled wound. The area around the wound was bright red with dead pieces of grey skin. The entire leg was still purplish.

"There's no hope, is there?" Sam asked as he looked at the damage.

"The most important thing is to keep infection away."

Kate glanced at Ryan, whose expression was scared again. She couldn't tell him the truth in front of her. Sam followed her gaze.

"Come here, Ryan, and hold my hand," he told her. "I might cry when your mom pours the medicine on."

Ryan scrambled over quickly. She leaned against Sam's chest and took his hand. His other hand went to her hair and smoothed his fingers over it.

"You won't tell anyone if I cry, will you?" he teased.

"It's our secret," she whispered against him.

"Do it," he said.

Kate decided to pour half of the contents on the wound. If she did it slowly, the pain could grow where he couldn't take it anymore, and she would need to stop. She was too worried about infection at this point.

Sam cried out, and Ryan clasped her arms completely around him. His head lifted and then sank back against the pillows.

"I've got you, Daddy," Ryan told him.

"I know you do." It came out strangled, and his fingers shook when he smoothed her hair again.

Kate wiped the surrounding skin gently and cleaned the wound as best she could. Sam remained stoic and didn't make a sound after his first outburst. Ryan hummed softly and rocked slightly.

By the time Kate finished, Ryan was asleep.

With a little help from Sam, Kate moved Ryan to a cushion she pushed beside him.

"She told me she fell into the water," Sam said once Ryan was settled.

Kate sat on the floor beside them. She covered her eyes with her hands at the memory.

"I thought it got her. I still can't believe it attacked seconds after she was out of the water. I never want to go through something like that again." She looked into Sam's eyes. "It's hunting us. I know that sounds ridiculous, but this is not normal shark behavior." She took a breath. "I've been thinking."

"That's dangerous," he said lightly.

Kate was hopeful that if he were joking, he was improving. She'd been thinking a lot about what she needed to tell him about the shark. The idea was crazy on the surface, but each layer worked when you considered their present circumstances.

She gave him her shark theory, which helped work it through in her head again. "Male great white sharks have known to travel and hunt in pairs. At first, I thought the shark in the net might have been a meal for the shark that bit you. I think this one, as stupid as it sounds, is out for revenge against the yacht."

"I was right. Your thinking is dangerous."

"The shark looked me in the eyes again, and its stare did not feel curious. It was exactly like the one who spy-hopped. What if that shark is the one that bit you? Maybe the shark in the net lived for a while caught beneath the boat. The other shark followed us and now blames our boat for its friend's death."

"And it wants revenge?" he asked skeptically.

"I know it sounds ridiculous."

As if it knew about their conversation in the galley, the shark chose that second to hit the hull again.

"Or maybe," Kate said, "it's hungry, and we just happen to be the ready meal on board."

"Out of the two of us, you're usually the more rational. Is there something you're not telling me?"

There was. Kate explained what her father said about the missing teens. "That attack wasn't normal either."

"You think this could be the same shark or same two sharks?" he asked. He no longer sounded doubtful.

"It's crazy, but something strange is happening. White sharks have been known to attack boats and tip smaller boats over, but it's very rare. The teens and now us. It just seems too coincidental for it not to be the same sharks."

"Do you think the coast guard will find us?"

Kate chuckled. "You know my father. If they don't, he'll come out himself if he isn't already searching. I'm going to go outside and shoot off another flare, just in case."

He took her hand.

"I love you," he said.

"I love you too." She covered his hand with her other one. "Don't forget that."

Kate wheeled herself to the deck and shot off a flare, knowing Ryan would be disappointed she slept through it. She glanced at the water and turned her head in the direction of a long distance splash off the starboard side. The shark just had to remind her it was still out there.

But then, in the distance, she heard the haunting call of the blue whale. A deep, melancholic moan that echoed the mysteries of the oceans. They were the lowest-frequency sounds made by any animal on earth and traveled for hundreds of miles underwater. Blue whales were highly endangered, and hearing this sound was special. The call was a poignant reminder of everything Kate loved about the endless depths of the ocean.

For some reason, the sound cemented in her mind that she was smarter than any damn shark.

17

DAY EIGHT, MORNING

F our days had passed since the shark attacked Sam. Throughout the night, Kate wrestled with his escalating temperature, employing wet towels and Tylenol. The last two hours were a harrowing vigil as she observed him shivering uncontrollably. Her hope that they would be rescued in time to save Sam was dwindling.

The relentless need to kill the shark consumed Kate's mind. She had extensive shark knowledge and concentrated on devising a plan. The creature stalking them exhibited relentless aggression, charging the boat almost hourly. Kate's ideas, though often seeming ridiculous, led to potential solutions, and she left no possibility unexplored.

Great whites had to swim to keep water passing through their mouth and out their gills to collect oxygen. She concluded that drowning the shark was the only viable option and to do that she had to stop it from swimming. Shooting a spear through its dorsal fin was the first step. She would then target its eyes—a vulnerable spot due to the lack of eyelids. The implements onboard were not the best but the smelly thawed meat would make a good bait to distract the shark.

They ate the last of the eggs for breakfast. Sam requested coffee, which she considered a positive sign after the night he had.

"You're deep in thought," he said after taking a sip and resting the mug on his lap.

"I want to kill the shark," she told him, speaking softly while Ryan played with plastic marine animals.

He took another sip before handing her the mug. She rested it beside her.

"Help will get here today," he said with confidence Kate didn't feel. "We'll be long gone before the shark knows it."

She couldn't return his smile. The lessons she learned from her father, while aboard boats when she was young, told her it would get worse before things got better and all she could do was prepare.

"I think we'll be rescued today too," she said. "I also thought that yesterday. We need to keep Ryan safe, and to do that, I'm being proactive."

She told him her thoughts on possibly injuring the shark or killing it.

"The anchor needs to be pulled up and redropped anyway. I can use the chain and possibly tie the spearfishing line to it. With his size, he can tow the anchor, but I was thinking maybe I could secure him to the side of the yacht where he would drown."

"Maybe we should just leave him alone," Sam suggested.

"This is the backup plan. We have the Sea-Doo, which I could use to go for help. I would carry an extra gas can to make it to another boat or the coastline," she contemplated aloud. "I would need to be strapped on, but I could do it just not with the shark out there."

"What if I went?" he asked.

She looked at him, and sadness filled her. She cupped his cheek. "You're not in good enough shape. If we're not rescued today, I'm taking out the shark, and then we can figure out the rest."

The shark hit the boat again.

"He doesn't give up," she said, feeling helpless once more.

"Come here." Sam pulled her against his chest. "We will get out of this and have a great story to tell our grandchildren."

For Kate, the contact was exactly what she needed. She loved this man so much. She would insist they go to couples therapy, which Sam had asked for in the beginning, and she had refused. They would come out the other side with a stronger marriage, and she would no longer stand in the way of healing.

She squeezed him back and simply rested against him for several peaceful minutes.

"Ryan and I need to wash and change. We have a good system for bringing up the water from the engine room. Would you like another bed bath?"

"Honestly, I need to sleep again. Even the coffee isn't keeping me awake."

She didn't mention he only took three small sips. Kate smiled against his chest, enjoying their closeness. His skin was thankfully cool. Sam squeezed her before he relaxed his arms, and she wiggled away and hoisted herself to her wheelchair.

"Come on, Ryan, we need soap, water, and a bristly brush to get the stink off you."

"Mooom," Ryan complained.

"Hey, you said I was stinky yesterday. I'm just returning the favor."

Sam was chuckling softly when they left the galley.

Using the same procedure that had been working for them, Kate sat on the floor at the hatch and helped Ryan downward as far as she could.

"Mom." The one word sounded worried.

Kate scooted closer and poked her head down the hatch.

"There's water on the floor," Ryan said and pointed the solar light downward.

Fuck. It was a word she never thought or used until now, and thankfully, she said it in her head and not aloud. She took a calming breath so Ryan couldn't hear the worry in her voice.

"Come on up, and we'll get the bath water later."

"Is the shark going to eat us?" Ryan asked when she was sitting next to her mom.

"No way. Why do you think I got the spearguns out?" Kate replied. "That shark will not hurt you. Your father will protect you too. We have the Sea-Doo and a life raft if we are really desperate. People are looking for us, and today is the day."

"I'm scared."

Kate turned slightly and placed her hands on the sides of Ryan's face, looking her straight in the eyes.

"I won't lie to you. This is scary, but I promise, the shark will not get you. The yacht can take on a lot of water, and we also have an emergency bilge hand pump for times like this when the power goes out."

"There are sharp knives in the galley too," Ryan said.

"Exactly, and we need to be thinking about those things. If we plan for every situation, we'll be ready for whatever that stupid shark does."

Ryan wrapped her arms around her mother's neck. "It is a stupid shark."

One disaster averted. Thankfully, Ryan had no idea how terrified Kate was. Her best guess was three inches of water in the engine room. The shark had discovered a weakness in the hull and exploited it.

Her family's time was running out.

DAY EIGHT, AFTERNOON

Kate located the bilge pump in the supply cabinet. She didn't have anything long enough to measure the amount of water in the engine compartment so she had to convince Ryan to go back down there and do the measuring.

"The shark could get me," she said, her eyes wide with genuine fear.

The knocks against the underside of the yacht had been unrelenting for the past hour. It was like the shark thought that it would eventually be able to swim through the hole it made. Her nerves on edge, Kate dismissed the absurd thinking. She despised the fact that her five-year-old daughter had to act in her stead. Life was unjust, and this was one of those moments when the harsh reality of her disability became painfully clear.

Kate took Ryan's hand. "I really need you to do this for me," she implored, looking directly into her daughter's eyes. "I would never put you in danger. The shark cannot reach you down there," she added, leaving unsaid the word, 'yet'.

Ryan brought her fists to her eyes to wipe away the tears she seldom shed. Kate's heart fractured a bit more with the gesture. She kissed her daughter's temple and provided light with a solar lamp as Ryan descended the ladder.

"Put your hand in the water with your fingers straight and gauge how high the water is."

"I did it, can I come back up now?"

"Get up here, silly."

Ryan's relieved smile when her head popped out of the hatch did little to assuage Kate's concerns about their predicament, but she was immensely proud of her daughter for facing her fears.

"It came up to here," Ryan said, extending her hand to indicate an imaginary water line that hit the middle knuckle.

This was a better outcome than Kate had anticipated. Thankfully, the hose was long enough to stretch down to the water from the top of the hatch where Kate stationed herself. Operating the pump was akin to using a handheld bicycle pump. She directed the expelled water into the bucket that was now positioned beside her on her wheelchair's seat. When the bucket was half full, Ryan wheeled it to the bathroom to empty it into the sink. The gray water drained into a tank that could be discharged into the ocean by flipping a switch in the engine compartment. Kate knew she would need Ryan's assistance again later, but for the moment, they had managed the situation.

As they labored, the shark intensified its attacks on the yacht, striking with almost rhythmic regularity. Despite Kate's efforts, she couldn't shake the notion that the shark had a goal and it was steadily achieving it.

They managed to pump out about an inch of water over the next hour. When Kate felt comfortable that they had removed enough, she had Ryan fetch her logbook so she could record the time and the volume of water they had removed. This would allow Kate to monitor the situation as closely as possible. After they finished, Ryan happily shot off another flare. They stood on the deck waiting again until it became too disheartening for Kate to bear.

She woke Sam to administer more Tylenol and another painkiller. He was groggy and irritable, and when she accidentally jostled his leg, he snapped.

"Dammit, what are you trying to do?" he exclaimed, his face flushing as he inhaled sharply.

Having full memory of her outbursts in the months following her accident, Kate remained composed. "I know it hurts. The pain medication will kick in soon," she reassured him.

"I'm sorry," he muttered after a few moments, his pain subsiding.

"Don't worry, I understand." She offered him a bottle of water. He took a small sip, his lips cracked and his skin parched from dehydration.

They needed assistance—and soon.

"Where's Ryan?" he inquired.

"She's in her bunk watching *The Little Mermaid* on my laptop which hopefully has enough battery power that she can finish it," Kate said.

"There's something you're not telling me," Sam said, gripping her hand. "We're going to get through this. What's happening?"

Kate couldn't conceal the truth any longer, but she knew that Sam would feel even worse knowing he was unable to help.

"The shark has been ramming the hull repeatedly. We discovered a little over two inches of water in the engine compartment. Ryan and I have managed to pump it down to an inch, but I'm unsure how quickly it's accumulating," she explained, giving him a moment to absorb the information. "If the damage to the hull worsens, we're in serious trouble."

"How the hell is he doing it?" Sam asked, his voice tinged with anger.

"He seems to be targeting a specific weak spot," Kate replied. It was impossible to believe they were having this conversation.

Sam's hand remained on hers, offering a silent gesture of support.

"What's your plan?" he finally asked.

"I'm back to considering the Sea Doo. If I had Ryan throw some spoiled meat overboard to distract the shark, I could attempt to get help," Kate proposed, though she was not fully convinced by her own suggestion.

He shook his head in disagreement.

"I'm aware it's not the best plan," she admitted, frustration evident in her voice. "I'm concerned about you. You need medical attention urgently, and time is running out. The shark is fixated on the yacht, and it won't stop. Taking the life raft would be tantamount to a death sentence with that shark lurking, and we can't take that risk. What if it's after us and not just the yacht?" Kate exhaled, grateful for the opportunity to voice her thoughts, even though Sam seemed hesitant about the idea.

"I can take the Sea Doo, and you stay with Ryan," Sam suggested.

"That's not feasible, and you know it," Kate countered, her voice heavy with regret.

"I have one functional leg. You have none," he pointed out bluntly.

The stark reality of his words stung, but Kate understood he didn't mean to hurt her. Sam's grip tightened as he looked intently into her eyes. She averted her gaze, finding solace in the blank screens of the control console.

"Kate, look at me," he urged.

Tears welled as she turned back to face him. "I'm clutching at straws," she admitted. "The Sea Doo plan is stupid."

"No, it's not," he insisted, his tone firm. "We can manage my pain, and I can do this. You wouldn't have considered this option if the situation weren't so dire. You're more capable of protecting our daughter here than I am. You need to stay with her."

Kate rested her head against his chest, comforted by the steady rhythm of his heartbeat. His hand soothingly stroked her back.

"I never truly fought for us," he whispered, his voice laden with regret. "I loved you and Ryan, but I often felt like an outsider, and that was my own doing. I'm an adult; I didn't need to be the center of attention. The affair was entirely my fault. It felt wrong from the start, and I felt unworthy of the love from my family. My shame has been a barrier, but I'm ready to fight for what matters most."

Kate remained silent, absorbing his words.

"I will take the Sea Doo and fight for us. Ryan can't look after me if my condition worsens before rescue arrives. This is the only viable solution. Do we need to act immediately?"

"No," she replied, her mind slowly accepting the idea of him leaving for help. The thought of not being the one to go, left her feeling numb at the prospect of him facing the dangers on the Sea Doo. Sam was correct though; if he were to die and leave Ryan alone on board, Kate could never forgive herself. "Tomorrow," she added after a pause. "We'll assess the water level overnight and make a final decision in the morning."

"I'm the one who will go," he stated decisively.

She embraced him tightly. "I know."

Over the next hour, she prepared Ryan for bed and launched another flare. "Mom gets the middle tonight," she announced to Ryan, ensuring there was space for her beside Sam. For the first time in two years, she slept within the security of his embrace. The positioning made it more difficult for her to check on the water in the engine compartment, but it was a small price to pay. When she returned to their makeshift bed, Sam drew her close, and they drifted back to sleep together.

As the early morning light filtered through the windows, a foot of water flooded the engine compartment overnight.

Day Nine, Morning

Kate prepared breakfast, deciding on a hot meal. She used three fuel cans to make cooking go faster. She opened a can of potatoes, diced them, and fried them. She also cut thin strips from one of the larger roasts, which had completely thawed, though it lacked the unpleasant odor of the other smaller meat choices in the freezer. Using the third fuel can, she boiled water and made enough coffee to get them through the morning.

She'd slept surprisingly well between the checks on the engine compartment and felt more in charge now. The doomsday feeling in the pit of her stomach also left and she looked forward to the large breakfast. She'd eaten more than Sam the past few days but not nearly enough so being hungry was a relief.

Even Sam managed to eat more food than he'd eaten since the attack though it exhausted him and he fell asleep shortly after finishing half his plate. Ryan had no problem gobbling her food. She even gave a small, unlady-like belch when she finished.

"Excuse me," she said and drank the last of her water.

She helped Kate clean the galley and get everything in its proper place. They were crowded enough with the seat cushions on the floor where they'd joined Sam for the meal and it was essential that Kate had room to move around.

The night flare from the previous evening had yielded no results. As disheartening as it was, Kate wouldn't give up; her family depended on her. She could pump water from the engine room herself, but she still needed Ryan to haul it to the bathroom, and worse, Ryan had to go down and flip the toggle that released the gray water into the ocean.

Scared and appearing as if she might throw up, Ryan voiced her fear, close to tears. "What if the shark breaks through?" she asked.

"I would never send you down if I thought the shark could get you," Kate assured her. "You are the most important person in my life and I will always protect you. If you can't do it, that's okay," Kate said, hugging her in reassurance.

Ryan took a moment to decide. Once the decision was made, her small shoulders pulled back, and her spine straightened.

"I can do it, Mommy."

The use of the words "mommy" and "daddy" showed the overall impact their predicament had on Ryan. She was holding herself together by a thread. Kate suspected Ryan didn't want her parents to know how terrified she truly was. The last thing Kate wanted to do was add to Ryan's stress, but she had no choice.

Kate felt the loss of her legs more now than at any time since the accident. She loathed her inability to help herself, and an unreasonable hatred for the shark grew with each passing hour.

"I'm ready, Mommy." Ryan's voice broke into Kate's moment of self-pity, and it was her turn to square her shoulders and show the same bravery her daughter displayed.

Ryan stepped down into the engine room slowly. Kate moved into position with her head over the hatch and held a solar light as soon as Ryan was on the floor.

"You've got this, Ryan. Mommy's here," Kate promised as her daughter tentatively placed a foot into the water in the engine compartment.

Ryan slugged along and followed Kate's directions until she found the correct switch. After her success, she splashed toward the ladder and launched herself up the steps in seconds, barely allowing Kate time to move out of the way.

"I did it," she cried and threw her arms around Kate. "I don't want to go down there again," she whispered.

"I'm so proud of you." She couldn't give Ryan the promise she wanted. Kate couldn't think of another reason to go down there, but she couldn't risk promising and then reneging. "Now I need your help hauling water. Does that work for you?"

Ryan nodded with relief.

It took two hours to remove another six inches of water. Kate had to face facts. A rescue team arriving in time looked more dismal with each passing hour. Sam's condition had deteriorated rapidly, and without medical intervention, he would die. If he were the one to take the

Sea-Doo, he would eventually fall off and drown. And no matter how she tried to play it in her head, he was the logical choice to go.

While she pumped the water, Kate tried to think of ways to make him safer, even though she knew she was fooling herself. Taking the Sea-Doo out was a huge risk, and she didn't feel good about it.

She pulled herself up to the main deck to speak with Sam and get his input.

"Duct tape," he said when she told him the Sea-Doo had to be used. "We'll tape my leg using a plastic bag so there's no blood in the water. I'll use your wheelchair to get to the Sea-Doo and send Ryan back for you before I take off. You and Ryan will toss meat off the platform and keep the shark's focus on an easy meal." He'd put as much thought into it as Kate.

"I'm still worried you'll fall off," she said truthfully. "We have some rope. What if we tied your hands to the handles?"

He thought about it before shaking his head. "I need my hands free to put more gas in the tank. If I feel unwell, I can slow down or even stop and rest. That's the worst-case scenario." He smiled to alleviate her worry, but she didn't return his grin. "Trust me, I can do this," he said, squeezing her hand.

She looked at him for a long time and then leaned in. His arms enclosed her, and her growing panic lessened. Sam would bring help back. This entire voyage would be a footnote in their life—an exciting one, but one they wouldn't want to revisit. Kate pictured them in side-by-side wheelchairs, wheeling their grandchildren around. A small grin tipped her lips up. She squeezed him extra tight.

"I need two pain pills to get out to the deck," he said after pulling back slightly. "I'll take added pills with me. Water, something salty to snack on, and extra gasoline for the jet ski will get this done. I'm sorry

I'm not much help. If you could get me the pills first, I want them to take effect before I move."

Kate worried two pills would make him groggy, but then decided not to argue. Adrenaline should keep him awake. It unsettled her stomach to think about what he was going to do. It would be easier if it were her.

"Have you told Ryan?" Sam asked when she returned with the pain pills.

"No." Kate had delayed it as long as possible.

"Send her in here; I'm the one who should explain what I'm going to do," he said.

"She's having a rough time," Kate admitted.

"I know. It's been so long since she's called me daddy; I'd forgotten that she had."

"I'll send her in," Kate said. She would give them time to say goodbye and for Sam to assure Ryan he would be okay.

While Sam and Ryan spoke, Kate stayed busy gathering the supplies he would need. She went onto the deck and examined the Sea-Doo. It was a high-end model; no part of Sam's body would touch water. It had a top speed of 65 miles per hour. Kate doubted he'd driven it that fast before, but the main goal was to get him far enough from the boat so the shark wouldn't care. Hopefully, the meat in the freezer would be the target.

She went back to the galley and ran into Ryan as she was heading to Sam's berth.

"Daddy wants his good luck hat that I got him for father's day," she said.

"That's a great idea. He definitely needs his lucky hat."

She wheeled up to Sam after Ryan ran off.

"She seems okay," Kate said.

"My leaving didn't go over well. The hat was a desperate measure, but I don't think the joy will last." He lifted his hand and Kate took it. "I promise to do everything in my power to save us. I'm sorry I haven't been any help up till now."

"That's ridiculous," she told him. "You took care of me for months. It's my turn, and besides, you get to be the hero and I'm slightly jealous."

He laughed and pulled her in for a hug. "I love you and Ryan. It will all be okay."

In his arms, Kate fully trusted that Sam would pull them from their real-life horror film.

20

Day Nine, Morning

Moving Sam to the Sea Doo was harder than expected. They took a break when his leg got jostled and he couldn't hide the pain. It was hard not to call off the crazy idea. Kate almost said exactly this aloud when Sam gave her the look. It had been a while since she'd seen it—I know what you're thinking and it won't matter.

He was as stubborn as her, reminding her of their earlier marriage. Until the affair, he had been opinionated and had no problem arguing when it was called for. His accommodating habits took over when he admitted to infidelity and became worse after her accident. Right now, he reminded her of the old Sam. She'd missed him.

By the time Ryan brought the wheelchair back, Kate was an emotional wreck. When she wheeled herself to Sam, he was pale and sweating. Even though his hand trembled, he lifted it in a halfhearted wave when he saw her.

"I'm okay, I just need a moment." He held her hand with his daughter leaning against his side in abject misery.

Ryan disliked the idea of him leaving them and she'd made her anger very clear. Her red and puffy eyes, appearing bigger than normal, held fear and her five-year-old brand of stubbornness. Ryan was in no mood for compliments and Kate would not dare mention how adorable she looked in her matching pink shorts and tee. Ryan stayed quiet in her self-imposed gloom with only mumbled replies when she couldn't get out of answering a direct question.

"I'm okay now," Sam said after a few minutes. "It's time to chum the water. Hopefully he'll gobble our prize roast and stay busy at the stern," he added in an upbeat tone for Ryan's benefit but received no response and turned back to Kate. "You can help me onto the Sea Doo as soon as he takes the bait." The shark chose that second to hit the underside of the yacht. "Let's get him out from under our boat." It was the needed rallying cry and even Ryan offered a small grin.

For the first time since the power went out, Kate felt proactive. Sam would find help and she would keep Ryan safe while he was gone. From the corner of her eye, she noticed that Ryan had moved to the rail and was holding her hand up, her shark tooth necklace dangling from her fingers.

"I hate you shark, but I'm giving you a tooth back so you'll feel better," she said in her little girl voice. She threw the necklace her grandpop gave her over the side and watched it sink. She turned back to her parents and stubbornly crossed her arms.

Sam winked at Kate when she looked at him.

"I believe she's more like you than your father," he said proudly.

No, Ryan was a combination of all three of them.

"She'll stay mad so hurry back," she said with a partial grin that was all she could manage.

"I'm set."

Kate examined him. She knew he hid his pain for her benefit. Regardless of his damp skin and the slight shake of his hands, Sam's eyes held determination. She had to let him do this, they had no other option.

Earlier she had cut up the rest of the roast they'd had for breakfast. She had placed half of it in the empty bucket when she finished and added more thawed meat to keep the shark busy. She'd left half of the meat in the freezer and placed the bucket on the deck beside the swim platform. Because of Ryan's fall into the ocean, she and Kate were attached to safety lines. They were set.

Kate left her wheelchair and settled on the casting platform at the bow. Ryan helped her lift the bucket before sitting next to her.

"Toss smaller pieces a few feet away," Kate said. "When we have his attention, we'll give him half the roast. After I help your father onto the Sea Doo, we'll feed him the rest." This would leave enough meat in the bucket to entice the shark after Sam took off.

Ryan looked at the bucket's contents and her tiny nose scrunched up before she pinched it closed. "It stinks," she said in a nasal tone.

"The stinkier, the better," Kate replied.

This received the first giggle of the morning. Ryan was five and sometimes she acted the part. She had her sullen moments but they never lasted long.

Kate tossed the first piece overboard and Ryan refused to be outdone and tossed the next one. They waited. Nothing.

"Again," Kate said, and they threw out more.

On the third round, the shark came to investigate. Its size was truly colossal especially for a male. Great white females grew larger though it was hard to contemplate anything bigger as the powerful creature coasted past them. It turned in a slow, easy manner and brushed the yacht with the side of its body. After making the pass, it returned for another one. This time when its head drew even with Kate and Ryan, it stared at them while continuing to drift past. Even though Kate knew the malevolence in the eye contact was in her imagination, she couldn't stop the shiver that spread across her exposed flesh on the warm day. She shook it off and tossed a larger piece of meat into the water.

The shark made a sudden strike toward the chum. The meat disappeared within its large jaws like it had never been there. The shark turned and its tail fin jolted the yacht with so much force it caused a splash that sprayed onto the deck.

Ryan fell slightly to her side when it happened. The safety line would not allow them to fall overboard but Ryan's expression held the terror from her earlier fall.

"It won't get you," Kate said. "Help me toss more in."

Ryan stared at her for a moment and made up her mind. She helped toss more meat over the side. The shark's behavior changed suddenly and it began to frenzy feed, grabbing meat it hadn't originally caught, rolling, and splashing.

"Now we help your father onto the Sea Doo." Kate scooted her butt to the inside edge of the platform and situated herself in the wheelchair. Ryan detached both safety lines so they could move to the stern.

"We have his attention," Kate said when she was next to Sam. She handed him one of the two-way radios so she could tell him when to leave. The radio would stay behind when he took off.

Getting him on the Sea Doo was painful and almost as hard as getting him on deck, but he managed to stay silent through the process. Ryan decided to be angry again and she simply stood back and watched.

"You need a moment," Kate told Sam when he was situated. Sweat covered his brow and his skin appeared gray in the sunlight. He breathed out then took in short gasps of air for a minute. They adjusted his leg and Kate checked the makeshift bandage covered in duct tape. She saw no signs of blood. When he was finally able to give a thumbs up, Kate unlatched the bar that held the craft.

"I've got this," Sam assured her and pulled his good luck, floppy brown hat down so it wouldn't fly off. He reached over and smoothed Kate's hair from her face. "Take care of Ryan, and I will see you both soon," he promised. "I'll start the engine when you signal you have the shark engaged." He hesitated and the look in his eyes changed. It was the old Sam, the one who always fought for his family. "I love you. We'll get through this and put our lives back together. No shark will stop us."

Kate grabbed his hand and squeezed. "I love you too." She added a bit of pressure. "Be sure to call my father."

"Got it. Come here, my little mermaid," he told Ryan.

She stayed still for about three seconds before running into her father's arms. He held her close and whispered something in her ear that made her giggle. Kate looked on with a sad smile. Dealing with Ryan while Sam went for help would be no fun. Kate would need to keep her busy. She looked up to see Sam watching her.

"Let's do this," he said, the strain of the past hour written in every line of his face.

Kate had smeared sunblock all over him and when she'd done it, she had noticed his weight loss. The dark circles beneath his eyes had grown worse. But Sam, her Sam, would never give up.

Carrying the two-way, Kate and Ryan made their way to the bow, reattached their safety lines, and situated themselves on the casting platform again. The shark hadn't gone under the yacht, he was waiting. Kate tossed a chunk of meat over the rail and he charged it.

"He's here," she called over the radio.

"I'll start the engine," Sam said. "If he leaves to investigate, tell me." The Sea Doo's engine rumbled to life, and thankfully, the shark stayed with them, more interested in feeding than the machine as Sam revved it.

"He's still here," Kate said over the radio. "I'm going to toss him half the roast, and you're good to go."

"I'm ready."

Kate lifted the heavy piece from the bucket and threw it into the water. The shark went after it immediately, and she gave the news to Sam. They heard him take off, and Kate tossed the other half of the roast in.

"Keep giving him small pieces," she told Ryan then looked in the direction Sam had taken and watched for a moment. She turned back around and glanced at the water. The shark was gone. "Throw more meat," Kate said urgently. They watched the bait float slightly and start sinking, but the shark didn't come for it.

"I'm getting down," she told Ryan. "You will stay here to keep tossing meat into the water," Kate said. Crap. She was breathing too fast and panicking. Ryan had noticed. Her eyes scanned the water, her expression filled with terror. The Sea Doo picked up speed giving Kate hope. She had no way of letting Sam know that the shark could be heading in his direction.

"Mommy," Ryan said shakily.

"Do what I say," Kate snapped. "Take this radio, and I'll get the one your dad left."

"Okay," was the pathetic tear-filled reply, but Kate was too busy fighting the safety line to pay attention. Her fingers slipped off the clip and she had to clumsily grab it again before she was free. The entire time she examined the water, looking for a dorsal fin. Slight waves from the Sea Doo rocked the yacht. She wheeled herself frantically toward the stern.

"Can you see the shark?" Kate asked her daughter over the radio when she stopped at the dive platform.

"No."

Sam was almost a hundred yards out, and there was no sign of the shark. Kate thought of the flare gun. Maybe if she shot it off, Sam would head back to the boat. Stupid thought because at this point it would be more dangerous. She watched with mounting hope as he hit the throttle again.

Everything changed.

The shark breached.

DAY NINE, MORNING TO MIDDAY

T ime slowed as the shark's massive body soared from the water. It appeared from the right, ensnaring Sam in its enormous jaws before plunging back into the ocean with a tremendous splash. Kate stared in disbelief, the scream dying in her throat, as she watched his hat drift slowly downward and settle on the water.

The shark had gone deep into the ocean so it could gain momentum for the breach. This was how they hunted. There was no record of a great white breaching on a human.

Until now.

The water stopped churning, and the silence was deafening. Sam did not come back up.

The realization entered Kate's mind that the shark was not after their boat; it was after her family, and it had just killed Sam. She had no air in her lungs, and she couldn't breathe. She bent forward, curling her upper body into a ball, terror eating at her insides. She wanted to die.

She had no idea how long she stayed that way.

Ryan.

The thought of her daughter brought her out of momentary paralysis. She turned her wheels toward the bow and stopped. Ryan stood a few feet behind her. Urine ran down her legs and pooled on the deck.

She'd watched her father die.

Kate wheeled toward Ryan, who remained frozen in place. Kate scooped her into her lap and held her as tightly as she could, the breach replaying in her mind again and again.

Ryan hadn't made a sound, and she was stiff in Kate's arms until she started trembling. Or maybe it was Kate shaking; she wasn't sure. For a short time, the world stopped. Her ears weren't taking in anything but white noise, her mind refusing to accept what she'd just seen.

They stayed that way until the shark hit the underside of the boat. It was her wake-up call. She had to kill it. Death for that monster was the only way to save her child.

Sam. Oh God, Sam.

She picked up the meat bucket because they needed it to bail the water. With Ryan on her lap, she wheeled them to the galley where Sam had lain for the past few days. Kate looked toward the control center, and the memory of Sam standing there, steering the yacht, looking so accomplished after his many training sessions, almost made her lose what little control she had.

Ryan mattered now. Sam gave his life so Ryan would live, and Kate would make damn sure their child survived. Ryan's small hands were clenching her, and a tiny whimper passed her lips. What could Kate say?

Once she could control herself, she started speaking in a low, soothing voice. "Grandpop is coming for us. We're going to be okay." She rubbed her daughter's back slowly, in small circles. She continued speaking. Ryan remained silent until Kate said, "I'm going to kill the damn shark myself." This was the first time Ryan heard her mother swear, and Kate didn't care.

Ryan wiggled a bit so she could look up at her mom. Her lips quivered, but her words were as strong as Kate's. "I'm going to kill it too."

Kate squeezed her tighter. "We'll do it together. Your grandpops will find us, and we'll go home."

Maybe an hour passed. Kate could feel slight pressure on her bladder, which meant she would wet herself if she didn't use the restroom soon. She also needed to get Ryan into new clothes. Kate's lap was damp with pee, but it would dry, and Kate didn't care about herself. The shark had continued hitting the yacht, and Kate needed to bail water in the engine compartment after the bathroom trip.

The smell of the rancid meat made her nauseous so she placed it in a large pan and shoved it into the freezer. She wheeled to the lower hatch with Ryan on her lap and explained what she needed to do.

"No, Mommy, I don't want to go down there."

"It's okay, sweetie, I promise," Kate assured her. "First the bathroom."

"Okay." It was whispered so softly Kate barely heard. She made it down the hatch and into her lower wheelchair. Ryan came down next and then held tightly to her arm as Kate wheeled herself to the bathroom.

"You can come in with me," she told her daughter at the door. Ryan nodded and followed her inside, which made it a tight squeeze. When Kate finished and sat back in her wheelchair, she took her daughter's hand.

"Bring me a new pair of shorts and change yours," Kate said. "Can you do that?"

Ryan didn't respond but she released Kate and walked away without complaint. She returned a few minutes later wearing a new pair of shorts. With a little help, Kate changed into the shorts Ryan brought. Ryan wrapped her arms around Kate and held on so tightly, breathing was difficult.

"If you want to help me kill the shark, I need you to be brave," Kate said and pulled away so she could look into Ryan's eyes.

There was a slight list to the port side of the yacht caused by the partially flooded engine compartment. As the engine room filled with water, the yacht would sink lower and listing would be more of a problem.

"We need to remove as much of the water as we can," she explained to Ryan. "You don't need to go down the hatch to the engine compartment again, but I need you to wheel the water bucket and dump it in the toilet."

Ryan nodded. Kate didn't give her time to think about it and wheeled straight to the engine room hatch. She sat on the floor and began pumping after a quick look. She estimated there was more than two feet, and pumping enough to make a difference would take time.

Ryan wheeled the water to the bathroom and came back without saying anything. Kate saw her tears but didn't mention them. Survival was all Kate could think of right now. Coddling Ryan would do neither of them any good. It took almost three hours to remove enough water so they were in the safe zone again.

Kate's next move was to feed Ryan, though she herself felt she would vomit if she tried to eat. The image of the shark grabbing Sam wouldn't leave her spinning head. She doubted it ever would. She felt empty, but the spark of determination that came with motherhood, was roaring to life.

"I'll make you anything you want," Kate said in a cheerful tone she didn't feel. Ryan shrugged. "If you don't tell me, it's peanut butter and jelly." Ryan shrugged again. "Peanut butter and jelly it is. We'll add chips and an apple if you want one."

Ryan stared at her. "How are we going to kill the shark?" While Kate had to think like a mother and also take out the shark, her daughter had a one track mind.

Kate hugged her. "I have a plan, and I'll tell you about it while we eat." At this point, Kate had to be as honest with Ryan as she could though she wouldn't tell her everything yet. The problem Kate feared the worst would send Ryan over the edge.

"A great white shark must continue swimming or it drowns," she said, as they ate their lunch. "The only way I can think of to stop it from getting oxygen is to secure it to the side of the yacht." Ryan's eyes opened wider, her body stiffened, and she slowly shook her head. "We have fishing hooks and spearguns to hold it," she explained and Ryan relaxed. "We'll tie the shark up so it can't get away, but we'll need to hook and spear it multiple times." Kate's end game if her plan with the fishing line didn't work was to use the anchor chain. She had to bring the anchor up first though.

"I miss Daddy," Ryan said and placed her head on Kate's lap.

Kate took a few minutes to run her fingers through Ryan's hair. If she offered verbal comfort, she would start crying and if she started, she didn't think she would stop. She lifted Ryan's face and kissed her before giving her another hug and releasing her.

They finished eating, and went back on deck, though Kate only had a few chips. She didn't look toward the stern where the Sea Doo usually rested. She couldn't.

The first step in releasing the anchor from the sea floor was attaching the anchor ball. The ball was for just-in-case scenarios like the one Kate and Ryan were in now. It helped release the anchor from the ocean bed if they didn't have power to run the electric winch.

The biggest problem was she needed to get to the end of the platform on the bow to reach the anchor locker. Kate had to get out farther than the safety line allowed, so she only attached one to Ryan. When her daughter was secure, she scooted from her chair to the platform.

"You need to stay here while I attach the ball," she told Ryan who grabbed her around her legs and buried her head in her lap. She wouldn't let go.

"Ryan, look at me," Kate said after a moment. Ryan didn't look up, and Kate had to pry her arms from her legs and push her back. "Ryan, you need to do exactly what I say. If you want to help me kill the shark, this is what we need to do. If you can't help, go back to the galley and wait for me."

Her child's eyes were desolate and at the same time filled with fear. Kate couldn't be nice. They had one chance, and Kate needed that chain. Ryan was losing her resolve, and terror was setting in. Kate took hold of her shoulders and squeezed to the point of pain. She had to bring Ryan out of the hell she was in long enough to help her.

"Mommy," stumbled from her lips that started quivering again.

"Ryan," Kate said sternly. "You must listen and understand. Stay here and keep hold of the rail. You can see me the entire time. I have a rail to hold onto also. I just need to slip the anchor ball on." She didn't give Ryan time to object as she started sliding on her butt toward the locker. She didn't turn to watch Ryan because it was breaking her heart to see her daughter this way.

Once she could grab the rope that held the chain, she placed the anchor ring around the rope and attached the anchor ball to it. She was ready to scoot back after tossing the ball into the ocean when the yacht started shaking.

"Mommy," Ryan screamed as she held the rail.

Kate managed to grab the closest rail and keep herself from pitching into the ocean. The shark was mouthing the swim platform with more anger than curiosity this time.

"Don't move," Kate yelled. "I'm staying here until it stops."

Ryan closed down again, her eyes going blank, as she held the rail with both hands. The shark savaged the back of the yacht for an extended period of time. When it finally stopped, it hit the underside of the boat so they would know he hadn't given up. Kate's thoughts turned to the water in the engine room again. She couldn't help thinking the shark knew exactly what it was doing.

If she didn't stop it, the shark would kill them. She consciously refocused her attention on the anchor. The easiest way to pull it up was to use the yacht, which meant it had to be mobile. With the netting still wrapped around the propeller shaft, she might get little to no movement. But they had two propellers, and to pull up the anchor, she needed to circle the ball with the boat, and it might work. The burning smell Ryan reported from the engine room worried her.

One problem at a time, she reminded herself. The shaking stopped. Once Kate was back in her wheelchair, she moved close to Ryan and told her it was time to turn on the engine.

"Do you want to go with me?"

Ryan nodded.

Kate detached her from the safety line and lifted Ryan to her lap. When she was at the door, she finally looked toward the back of the yacht. Something in the distance caught her eye, and it wasn't the shark. "Ryan, go inside and carefully grab the flare gun. Can you do that?" She lifted Ryan from her lap.

There was a large cruise ship far in the distance. It might be aware that people were missing at sea. Ryan came out carrying the flare gun and handed it to her mother.

"Look out there," Kate said and pointed to the ship that was a tiny dot on the horizon. "Do you want to shoot the flares?" Ryan gazed at her, not understanding the significance of the ship. She was still in shock, Kate reminded herself.

After several seconds and no response from Ryan. Kate wheeled inside and grabbed the gun. She moved back to the deck, lifted it, and fired.

22

Day Nine, Afternoon

K ate fired twice, each shot about three minutes apart. She could swear her heart stopped during the interminable wait. She had no idea how much time had passed when someone on the cruise ship sent up an answering flare.

"Look." She smiled at Ryan. "They see us."

Ryan looked toward the disappearing cruise ship and saw the smoke trail from the answering flare.

"Will they come get us?" she asked, without an answering smile.

Kate tempered her excitement. Sam was dead. Their rescue was too late to save him. She wasn't sure what she expected, but it was disheartening to see the ship fade into the distance. Realistically, Kate knew they wouldn't turn their giant behemoth around and come to the rescue.

"They will notify the coastguard and give our exact location," she promised and hugged her daughter. Help was coming.

The shark chose that moment to attack the stern again. After his visible burst of aggression, he went to the underside of the yacht and hit it. The list to the port side had returned, which wasn't good.

Kate decided to remove more water from the engine compartment while they waited for their rescue. Ryan didn't object when Kate told her she needed help again. They made their way to the engine room ladder. Kate went to the floor to lift the hatch. What she saw caused a terrible realization.

The water line was three feet from the hatch, which meant they were going down fast.

The elation she felt at seeing the flare disappeared. They had a life raft, but with the shark present, it was unusable. Kate could not risk the boat sinking before help arrived.

"If we caught one break, now would be the time," she muttered to herself. "Change of plans," she told Ryan. "We need to go back on deck."

"Where they can see us?"

"Yes," Kate replied, without showing the fear that was sinking deep into her bones, clenching her heart, and making breathing difficult. With the water in the engine compartment at such a high level, she could no longer power up the yacht. She switched gears because keeping Ryan alive was all that mattered now. She could manually pull up the anchor, even though it wouldn't be easy. Hopefully, before she got too far into it, the coastguard would arrive.

She secured a safety line to Ryan and didn't make a big deal of it when she didn't attach her own. She took an extra rope from the container and placed it on the swim platform before she lifted herself off the wheelchair and scooted next to it. Ryan stood beside the casting platform, holding onto the rail. Kate dragged herself to the anchor line and secured the extra rope. She then started the slow process of dragging her legs behind her back to her wheelchair on the deck.

Once she was in place, she secured a safety line to her waist and pulled steadily on the rope. Slowly, the yacht turned, but the list worsened. Heavy shaking, coming from beneath them, rocked the boat. It seemed unbelievable, but the shark had created a tear in the hull that it was systematically enlarging.

They were taking on water much too fast.

Her thoughts focused.

Kill the shark.

Hand over hand, her arms aching, her entire body fatigued, she continued pulling as the sun beat down on the back of her head. Slowly, the yacht moved inch by inch until it gradually swung around. Her muscles screamed, her back ached, and she didn't stop until the boat faced the anchor.

"I need you behind me," Kate told Ryan, beyond exhausted, fighting the knowledge that she might not succeed. "Now," she said, once Ryan got into position, "pull on the rope as hard as you can."

Ryan wasn't much help, but it kept her arms moving and, hopefully, her mind occupied. With a deep shuttering groan, the yacht listed a few inches more. The starboard side would have been better for this, but the path her wheelchair would take wasn't as wide, and maneuverability was limited. For now, they would work with what they had.

They pulled for what seemed like hours when they finally hit the chain section. The anchor ball helped, but it really needed the boat to do the heavy work, and that wasn't happening. Kate took a few minutes to rest and think.

"Mommy."

The tremble in Ryan's voice alerted Kate to the shark. She glanced up and looked straight into the dark eyes that had killed Sam.

"Grab your safety line and move toward the cabin," Kate told Ryan.

The wheelchair was pushed against the rail by the list, and she didn't like how close the shark was. She glared into the malevolent eyes, her fear replaced by fury. This monster wanted to kill her child, and that would not happen.

Her rest break at an end, she continued hauling in the chain.

The shark went under. A moment later, she felt a strong pull in her grip, almost tearing it from her hands. The pressure stopped suddenly, and thirty seconds later, the anchor ball moved with such force, she knew the shark had it.

White sharks had high intelligence. Even with its size, great whites didn't become a top ocean predator by being stupid. What this shark was doing, however, was too much for Kate's sanity. The fear she'd been fighting ebbed its way back to the forefront.

To gain control, she mentally reviewed the shark's behavior so her mind could grasp what was happening: She pulled on the chain—the shark went after the chain. It would know she was trying to escape. That's what prey did. The shark wanted to keep her from getting away. It was as simple as that. There was no otherworldly force at play. It was a damn shark. It was real. It bled. It could die. With a deep inhale, she focused on the end game.

The hard plastic anchor ball popped up. The shark took it down again, but it came back up quickly. Ryan moved closer and tried to pull the chain with her mother, but she was unable to lift the weight.

"Grab the other safety line and tie it to the chain every few feet," Kate told her. Thankfully, one of Ryan's first boating lessons was tying knots, and she had several in her wheelhouse. "It will keep the chain from falling back into the ocean," Kate explained.

While doing as her mother asked, Ryan's eyes glanced fearfully at the water.

Kate's entire body trembled with strain as she steadily pulled on the seemingly endless chain. She didn't pay attention to the rising heat or the shark. She had to get to the anchor. Her arms and back had started cramping when the anchor ball began moving closer to the boat, and some of the weight lessened.

The shark attacked the ball again, causing another heavy pull on the chain. The yacht was pulled in the direction of the ball, not the other way around. The shark was pulling them. All Kate could do was loop the rope around the rail and wait it out. When the resistance stopped, she slipped the rope free and pulled again. When the anchor ball returned to the surface, it was a chewed-up mess, but somehow the shark had not severed the rope that held it in place.

Kate used more rope to form a slight pulley system using the rail to bring the heavy anchor to the boat's side. She used the same method to get the anchor onto the deck. It clanged when it slipped from her fingers and hit the ground. Kate bent double in her chair for a moment to get her breath back.

She opened her eyes, her gaze drawn to something in the water brushing against the hull. Kate leaned closer and saw the dark material. It hit the side of the boat again, sliding through the water and she realized what it was. Sam's hat, the brown material wet and appearing darker, the side flaps waving, a horrifying reminder of what happened to Sam. She almost lost the tight hold she had on her emotions. With a steadying breath, reverently, she released the hook pole from the side rail. She lifted it to the water and hooked the soggy hat and brought it to the deck. Her fingers closed on it and water dripped as she brought it to her lap. She didn't feel the cold wetness, she didn't smell the sea water. She saw her husband, the man he was when she married him.

Unable to hold back tears, she leaned forward and sobbed. A small hand settled on her back and light circles rubbed across her shirt. Kate grabbed desperately at Ryan and pulled her closer.

Snapshots frozen in time tumbled through Kate's mind, images of Sam cycling like a reel of photos. The one she grabbed onto was of him holding a newborn Ryan with tears in his eyes, so happy to be a father, so proud.

"We're going to be okay," she gruffly told Ryan. "I promise."

Ryan gave her another hug before her arms slipped away.

From the position of the sun, they had been working for around two hours, but she now had the key piece for her plan to succeed if the first part failed. It was time to check the water level below deck. She stuck the wet hat beneath her butt on the wheelchair, unwilling to part with it.

Kate was afraid of what she would find below and needed a reminder of Sam with her.

DAY NINE, AFTERNOON

"Stay on deck," Kate told Ryan before she transferred from the wheelchair to the floor, preparing to descend through the hatch to the lower level.

"Did the shark get inside?" Ryan's eyes, wide with unspoken fear, darted frantically from Kate to the hatch.

"No. I need to check the water level, and I'll be back up in a few minutes. It won't take long." She paused to study her daughter. "You can come if you want."

"I want to stay here." Ryan's words and tone conveyed she wasn't interested in going to the lower deck at all.

"I'll be right back." Kate decided that admitting the boat was sinking could wait a bit longer. It also needed to be worded so Ryan was part of the solution and she didn't have time to panic. She also knew her daughter was too smart for her own good and most likely knew they were in danger regardless of how much Kate wanted to keep things from her.

She maneuvered into the lower wheelchair and headed straight for the engine hatch. It wasn't submerged, a good sign. Lifting the door revealed the water had risen another six inches. She pondered whether to alter her plan and do everything possible to keep the yacht afloat until help arrived, or to stick with the plan to kill the shark. The animal would eventually take the yacht down. It was too big a risk to rely on others that may or may not arrive in time. Kate cranked the wheels of her chair. It was harder to navigate with the port side list, but she managed. She made it to the hatch and pulled herself up using the rope. The ache in her arms from hauling in the anchor and going up and down the hatch so often made it nearly impossible but there was no way she would give up. Her muscles would just need to handle the torture.

Ryan waited anxiously for her mother's return and gave a relieved sigh when she saw Kate.

"It's time to hook the shark," Kate told her after catching her breath.

"Are we going to kill it?" Ryan asked somberly.

Ryan had been taught by her grandpops to dislike people who harmed sharks. He gave no one, not even conscientious fishermen, a free pass. He had no problem teaching his loathing of those who didn't value the ocean to his granddaughter and he'd done a good job of it.

"We're going to catch it and let the boat do the work. Are you okay with that?" It wouldn't matter what she said, but Kate needed to know where Ryan's head was at.

Her expression grew thoughtful and her little nose scrunched up. "Grandpops would kill it," she decided with finality.

He would. If he were with them right now, he would have a better plan to do the job. Kate had no misconception that her father could and would do what it took to keep them safe. She was doing the same, and she had no moral dilemma about doing so.

This was life or death. She and Ryan *would* survive.

She'd spent so much time on boats, she understood what was happening to the yacht as it took on water. The deck, once steady was now treacherous. As the boat sank lower, it would get worse. Eventually, the ocean would swallow Ryan's Gift. Kate and Ryan could not be onboard when that happened and they could not have an angry shark waiting for them.

They secured their emergency lines as soon as they were on the main deck. The tilt of the yacht made the use of her wheelchair nearly impossible. She finally pulled on the outer rail to move herself closer to the container with the diving and fishing gear. The shark chose the moment she released the rail to hit the boat again. It startled her more than anything. This insistence on announcing his presence was getting on her last nerve.

The life raft came fully equipped for emergencies with food, water, flairs, and a few other essential items. Sam had upgraded the raft before their fateful journey began. Kate didn't waste time checking it. Time was not on their side.

She made it the final few feet to the containers and found the largest of the fishing hooks. They were around the size of her palm. She had no idea if they would work on a shark even half the size of this one but it's what she had. She knew as much about fishing as she knew about shark bites, which was next to nothing. She found a roll of 150 pound cable and a cutter for it. The immediate problem was keeping what she needed from falling overboard. She placed what she would use in the container with the spear guns and then went back to the diving gear. She removed her weighted diving belt and took out the weights. She then adjusted the belt around her waist and placed the hooks and wire cutter inside the empty pouches. She would need the net eventually but left it in the container for now.

Sam's belt rested inside too and she noticed the knife she'd had him take when he'd checked the propeller. She attached it to her belt. Kate had a vague idea of how her plan would work. The thought of failure made her nervous, but non action was not an alternative.

After closing the container lids, she wheeled back inside for bait. Ryan stayed next to her holding onto the side of the wheelchair. Kate had left the bucket in the galley. She used it to load the remaining meat from the freezer. The smell was worse than before and the meat had turned a not so lovely shade of gray. She sat the bucket down and pulled Ryan around so they were facing each other.

Her daughter's sweet face and trusting eyes stared back at her. Sam's eyes. Kate fought back tears again. She had to stay focused. She couldn't think about Sam and the life they should be leading. Even though she hadn't replied when he told her to keep Ryan alive, she'd made him a promise. The shark would not get to Ryan. It was her new mantra.

"This is important," Kate said. "I need you to do what I say, when I say it. If I send you in here, you won't question me. Okay?"

"Okay, Mommy." Tears filled Ryan's eyes. "If we kill the shark, will Daddy come up from the water so we can save him?"

The question startled Kate for a moment. Then she remembered discovering her father watched Jaws with Ryan. Kate had been so angry, but he'd laughed it off and told her it was a rite of passage. Matt Hooper, played by Richard Dreyfuss in Jaws, had swam out of the ocean at the end of the movie and hadn't died.

"I don't know," she said with an internal cringe because Kate couldn't tell her daughter the truth yet. Sam was not coming back, and she couldn't risk Ryan sinking into a place where she didn't react to what Kate said or needed. "We need to secure the shark. That's the most important goal right now."

Ryan simply nodded.

"Are you ready?" Kate asked.

Another nod.

It was time.

DAY NINE, AFTERNOON

The rank meat should catch the shark's attention. Once it came close and began eating, Kate would shoot multiple spears into its body. Her goal was to land at least one through the dorsal fin. There was a clip toward the end of the spear shaft that resembled a toggle bolt for a hollow wall. It worked the same way. If Kate could get the spear point through the meaty part of the dorsal fin, it would lock itself in place.

She'd never used a speargun before in her life. It had taken her longer than expected to figure out how the thing worked. Reloading would take time because, again, she wasn't familiar with spearguns. She also knew the cable wouldn't hold unless she hit the shark multiple times. An eye would be nice. And to top off all of this, Kate was firing a speargun out of the water. She had no idea what the ramifications would be. The trajectory could be off or it could be very dangerous for the person shooting it.

So many ifs.

"We'll do this from the starboard side," she told Ryan. "I won't be able to turn around, and I'll need your help. You will always stay in front of me. If we need to back up, you'll follow. If I move forward, you'll move first, understood?"

"Understood." Ryan's voice was firmer, and so was her head nod.

Kate thought of a way to secure what she needed so it was close at hand. The net would fit in her red backpack. She had Ryan empty the backpack's contents and add two bottles of water. Kate placed the pack in her lap and put the smelly bucket on top of it.

She was ready.

They moved to the deck, where the heat of the day was in full swing. Kate began setting up. She tied the spears to the 150-pound cable using wire she also found in the fishing container. She attached the end of the lines to the bottom T-brace that secured the guard rail to the starboard side of the boat leaving plenty of slack so the spear didn't pop back toward her if it missed. She rolled back, and Ryan handed her another spear. She attached the next line to a cleat, clipped the cable, and moved to the next T-brace. She was unsure what would hold the shark, so decided on a cleat and T-brace combination.

"Be sure to step over the wires so you don't get caught up in them," she told Ryan.

Kate attached five spears. Next, she took out the net and examined it. She may not have known much about spearguns or nets, but she knew this one was to catch bait fish. She needed the shark caught up in cable, rope, and netting for this to work.

Kate went through the mechanics of the speargun again to be sure she had it put together properly. Once she was satisfied, she moved to the hooks. She attached the wire cord to three of the four and dug her hand into the bucket and slid the rancid meat onto the hook.

"Uck," Ryan said.

Kate lifted her left hand, forming her fingers into bloody claws, and said, "Arrr."

"That's gross, Mom."

We were back to 'Mom', and Kate's feeling that Ryan's mind needed to be occupied right now was correct. Her daughter wasn't thinking about her father; she was thinking about killing the shark. Kate finished the other two hooks. She still had the roast and a few pounds of meat.

"There's enough left to chum the waters. I need to tie the hooks off first."

"What about the big fishing poles under my bed?"

So, that's what Sam did with the poles. Kate didn't really want them on board because they opposed fishing, but the previous owners didn't have their understanding of what overfishing was doing to the oceans. She and Sam hadn't removed the rod holders, and now Kate could use them.

They went back into the cabin, and this time Ryan didn't complain about going to the lower deck with her. She excitedly pulled the two poles out from under her bed.

"We need the biggest one," Kate said.

Ryan slipped the smaller of the two back into place and carried the larger one up the stairs while Kate used the rope again to gain the upper level.

Once the pole was secured in the rod holder, Kate attached the hook.

She mentally reviewed her plan. She feared it wasn't enough. Without the anchor in place, the yacht was drifting. She had no idea how far they would be from the coordinates the cruise ship would have on them.

Her thoughts went to the anchor and chain, which made her heartbeat ramp up. It might be the only solution, and it terrified her. "It's a last resort," she reminded herself.

The shark rhythmically hit the underside of the yacht, and the list was growing worse by the hour. The shark had a plan and it was systematically putting it into motion.

That was okay because Kate had a plan too.

DAY NINE, AFTERNOON

The shark made a sudden appearance on the starboard side just before Kate began chumming the water. The large head rose up slowly in another sky-hop. Kate's feeling for this particular shark had shifted. Perhaps all sharks were this intelligent, but the one-track mind of this one seemed off the charts. Once they were out of this situation, she and her father would have a lot to discuss. He spoke publicly about the intelligence of sharks and stingrays, and Kate was now experiencing the truth in his words firsthand.

She glanced at Ryan as the shark disappeared beneath the surface. "It's now or never," she declared.

Ryan responded with a definitive nod, though no words were exchanged.

"Are you willing to lend a hand and help me chum?" Kate asked.

Without hesitation, Ryan reached into the stinky bucket, pulling out a chunk of meat, and tossed it a few feet from the boat.

Kate stood by the side, watching as the meat slowly sank. It was there, and then all she saw were large jaws closing around it. The shark twisted, running its body along the hull, physically moving the yacht. Ryan tossed out another chunk.

"We need it to take a hooked piece the next time," Kate instructed after the shark grabbed the meat. She released the switch on the reel to allow the line to feed out if the shark caught it. She used the other hooks first, tossing them overboard at a similar distance to Ryan's throw.

This time, the shark appeared more curious, nudging the hooked meat without biting.

"Come on," Kate whispered as she lifted the speargun and loaded it. The shark swam past, the dorsal fin fully exposed. She fired.

The spear overshot the target and Kate wasn't surprised. She pulled in the line and thought about how to adjust for another shot.

"Move forward so I can turn the chair around," Kate told her daughter. She needed to face the back of the yacht. Ryan moved in front of her until they reached the bow and Kate could turn her chair to face the opposite direction. She backed the chair to the spot she'd been in before. Kate turned almost sideways at her waist to prepare for the next shot. She loaded the spear and aimed at the water. Then, she waited.

The shark took another pass before it returned for one of the hooked meats. When its jaws opened to taste, she fired again. The shaft entered its upper back. The shark showed no sign that it now had a spear lodged in it. She placed another spear and fired again. Another miss. She needed to slow down and time her pull on the trigger. She'd got him once but she needed to land the one in his fin to make this work. Her next shot missed too.

"Damn," she said and immediately looked at Ryan. "I shouldn't have said that."

Ryan glanced at her with old soul eyes and blinked. "If we kill it, can I say a bad word?" she asked, completely serious, no smile just an intense expression.

"Once," Kate replied. "But you need to wait until we're sure or you'll waste it." Allowing her daughter to say a swear word over what they were facing was definitely a Sam thing and not something Kate would ever do. Desperate times.

The shark thrashed, hitting the boat several times, splashing them with ocean water before it went under and attacked the hull.

"Toss another chunk out," Kate said.

It only took a moment for the shark to return to the surface. Kate was determined to hit the dorsal fin so she took her time. Ryan tossed another piece a bit farther away this time and the shark turned leisurely and headed to it.

Kate fired again. The spear passed through the dorsal fin in the perfect location.

"Yes!" she yelled but raised her hand to signal her daughter to wait. "Hold off on that bad word, it's not dead yet," she teased in excitement.

The shark thrashed, went under and returned within thirty seconds. Kate fired again, hitting it slightly above the tail fin. The shark disappeared.

Kate wheeled to the first hooked line and jiggled it, trying to entice the shark above the surface. It wasn't hitting the boat's underside because it probably didn't have enough line to reach the damaged area. She readied herself at the cleat. They waited with no sign of the shark.

"Where did it go?" Ryan asked.

"I'm not sure." Kate glanced at the water's surface trying to spot it but there wasn't so much as a ripple.

She handed Ryan a bottle of water from the backpack. The day continued warming. She rescanned the ocean. It stayed a smooth blue sheet of nothingness. They drank water as they waited.

The shark struck the yacht so hard, Kate's upper body flung forward and her head hit the middle rail. It was a solid strike and she lifted her hand to check for blood. Thankfully it came away clean and the world stopped warbling. The shark now had her full attention. It nudged a piece of meat with its snout. The line attached to the shark's fin remained taut for several minutes before it came closer and Kate could wrap it several times around the cleat giving it less maneuverability. When the shark turned, the yacht dipped on the starboard side and it was Kate's shoulder that hit the rail this time. Turning her upper body, she grabbed a terrified Ryan over the back of her chair and held on until the yacht rose again.

The shark sank below the surface so she couldn't see the bloody thing. A huge splash of water hit them and then the ocean went still again. The battle wasn't over and Kate grabbed the next spear, waiting for the perfect moment. The shark resurfaced, and she pulled the trigger, hitting above the eye.

"You did it, Mommy!" Ryan shouted.

The shark went into a frenzy which meant it felt that one. It was horrible of Kate to feel joy at the creature's pain but she didn't care. She unfurled the net, tied the end to the anchor rope, and threw it toward the shark. Even with it thrashing, the net connected, partially covering its head. Kate pulled and looped the line around the cleat as tight as she could. The yacht pitched dangerously while the shark tried to free itself.

"We need to move!" Kate shouted. "I'm going to detach your line and then mine. Don't let go of the chair."

With Ryan in back of her, holding on tightly, Kate wheeled toward the stern. The yacht lurched, water splashed, and the boat lifted and crashed back down. It tipped, and Kate's hand skimmed the water, dangerously close to the panicked shark.

"We're good," Kate assured Ryan, though her attention remained on the huge jaws that would give her nightmares for decades. It fought the cables, and it was only a matter of time before it freed itself.

The thrashing grew wilder. Holding onto Ryan and the rail, Kate fought to keep them out of the water. The yacht tipped. Kate knew the port side of the yacht had to be completely submerged because suddenly she was looking down on the shark.

"Mommy!" Ryan screamed as she flailed.

Kate's grip on the metal rail slipped.

26

DAY NINE, AFTERNOON

K ate's heart lurched into her stomach as she grabbed frantically
at nothing but air. With a huge splash, the yacht settled back
into the water, causing the wheelchair to ram into the side of the cabin.
Kate grabbed a safety line to stabilize herself and she was able to breathe
again.

A sobbing Ryan held onto her mother as tightly as she could. This
was it. Kate had limited time before the shark freed itself. She swiftly
pushed the wheels of her chair to the stern. The yacht continued rocking.

After Kate turned her chair to face Ryan, her daughter's head went into her lap, and both of Ryan's hands clung to Kate's shirt. The shark was not getting her daughter, but what needed to happen next would be unbearable for Ryan. Kate didn't see another way. The hooks were empty, and they were out of meat.

She cupped Ryan's cheeks and lifted her head so her daughter had to look into her eyes. Everything inside Kate rebelled at what she had to do.

"I need you to be strong for me," she said in a harsh tone and hated herself for it. Her voice leveled out with her next words, "I love you, and I know you can do this. The shark is going to break loose, and there's only one way to stop it."

Ryan's lips trembled, and she shook her head slightly, her fingers tightening and digging into Kate's stomach. "Listen to me," Kate said firmly. "You will do exactly as I say, do you understand?"

"I'm scared, Mommy." Tears flowed down her face, and there was nothing Kate could do to make this easier.

She took a few seconds to hug her daughter, hoping it wouldn't be the last time. Life could be cruel, and she hated that Ryan had to learn the lesson so young. She finally pulled back.

"We're both scared," Kate said. "It's okay. I'm getting the raft out so it's ready."

"No," Ryan said, her terror causing her small body to shake even more.

"We don't have a choice. The coastguard will come for us, but the boat might go down first. We need to be prepared. I'm going to make sure the shark can't get away from the boat, and it drowns quickly." Kate had been running what she knew about sharks dying from lack of oxygen through her head since the anchor idea came to her. From what she remembered, the larger the shark, the quicker it died from lack of oxygen. The shark continued thrashing, and the only explanation was that it had too much room to maneuver. Crap, it would break the cables that held it before she had it secured tightly enough.

She wheeled to the storage container that held the life raft, and with Ryan's help, she managed to drag it out. Kate pulled the thirty-foot inflation strap halfway out so it would be easier for Ryan if she had to inflate it herself.

"You keep pulling this until it won't go any farther." She quickly showed Ryan what she meant, while she panicked internally that the shark would be free before she could fully secure it. "The raft has everything you need. When you can't pull this anymore, you give it a hard tug. After it inflates, push the raft off the swim platform and climb into it. Okay?" The raft had several chambers that held air so if one leaked, it would still float.

Ryan's blank expression showed she wasn't keeping up. "How are you going to kill the shark?" she asked softly.

She was too smart for her own good, and Kate needed her to hold on mentally just a bit more. Then, Kate thought of something that would help.

"Shoot off another flare. We're drifting, and we want the coastguard to see us as quickly as possible." After a short hesitation, Ryan had no problem doing the task, and it distracted her, which was exactly what Kate wanted.

"Do you understand how the raft works?" Kate asked.

Ryan nodded uncertainly.

Kate secured her to a different safety line so she didn't need to worry about her going overboard.

"We're moving to the anchor," Kate said next.

She wheeled to where she left the anchor on the port side. With Ryan's help, they lifted it to Kate's lap. She managed to heft enough chain with it so she could reach the starboard side and still have plenty of length to work with. Kate tied a section of rope that she'd left secured to one of the rails and attached it to the chain close to the anchor. The yacht pitched high again, and Kate had to hold the rail. She struggled to wheel around the yacht to where the shark was trapped, but she made it and peered over the side. Dark eyes settled on her immediately. Her gaze locked with the shark's.

Animosity, vengeance, and determination hit Kate like strong waves from the ocean. It didn't worry her. She had her own vengeance to settle. The shark went into another frenzy and one of the spears came out. Time was on the shark's side, and sooner or later, it would be free. The next part of her plan had to work.

"We're going to swing the anchor high enough to go over the shark," Kate said. "It won't be easy."

"Will it stab him?" Ryan asked.

The anchor had dual points at the end, so it grabbed the sea floor. "No," Kate replied. "We want it over the shark's back."

Ryan didn't understand, and Kate didn't want her to until the last possible moment. The railing groaned, and Kate wasn't sure if the T-brackets would hold much longer. The cleats were starting to rattle too. She allowed the chain to slip from her lap until all she held was the anchor.

"We can do this," she told Ryan. "Stand next to me while I prop it on the rail." Kate's upper body was strong, but thirty-five pounds of ungainly weight would not be easy to toss far enough. Slowly, using the upright post against the anchor as a guide, she lifted it until the weight teetered on the middle rail. The anchor almost slipped and went into the water, but Kate managed to hang on. Refusing to consider the ache in her arms, she was ready.

"When the shark's body is alongside the hull, we'll try to toss it," she told her daughter.

"The shark went under again," Ryan said warily while peering into the water. She had one hand gripped tightly to the arm of Kate's chair and the other holding her safety line.

The yacht groaned and dipped. Kate was sure the water from the engine compartment had reached the berths. The yacht was going down, and the shark was still alive. They may not have another chance.

"He's up," Ryan yelled.

"Here we go. Push as hard as you can on three." Ryan placed both hands on the anchor. "One, two, three," Kate said as she grunted with effort. The anchor hit the shark in the back and seemed to stun it for a moment. Unfortunately, Kate knew it hadn't caused lasting damage. The shark sank down, and she couldn't see it in the murky water. Kate wasn't sure if the anchor was out far enough to do what she needed. The weight of the anchor pulled the chain off the deck until one of the ropes attached slid into the water too.

When the shark finally came back up, the rope was on the far side and not between the shark and the boat. She pulled on the rope until the chain hit the sharks side and she could secure it tighter. The first part of her plan had worked. Now she had to act fast. Kate took hold of Ryan's shoulders.

"Listen to me," she said. "I need to go into the water. You know how to inflate the life raft. If I don't come back up, that's what you will do. Okay?"

Ryan stared at her and then began to slowly shake her head.

"Ryan. I need you to tell me you understand."

"No," Ryan whispered. "It will eat you."

"No, it won't. It's still caught by the spears. I won't get close enough to it, but I need to grab the rope tied to the chain and bring it up on the port side where we can tighten it and the shark won't be able to escape."

"Mommy, no." Ryan grabbed onto Kate frantically.

Kate took hold of her fingers and pried them away, holding Ryan's hands in hers. "I know this is scary, but the boat is sinking, and we need to get into the raft. In order to do that safely, the shark must be secured to the boat. I love you." She pulled her sobbing daughter into her arms. "I'm going to come back, I promise."

Ryan's small shoulders shook uncontrollably and her cries twisted Kate's heart. She had to go through with her plan to keep her daughter alive. Kate checked the rope attached to the anchor to make sure it was secure. She then lifted Ryan into her arms and moved the wheelchair forward until she circled around the stern and stopped where she left the raft. She tied it off on a cleat, ready to be inflated. Ryan clung to her. Once the raft was tied using a slipknot, Kate turned around and went back to the stern. When she tried to place Ryan on the deck, she cried out and held tighter. Kate glanced at the water behind them. The shark still had spears attached, but Kate knew she had minutes to make sure it couldn't escape.

She forcefully separated Ryan from her and Ryan started screaming.

"Ryan, stop," Kate yelled as she swung from the wheelchair to the deck.

"Mommy, please don't go, please."

Kate was barely paying attention to Ryan. She hated this, but it was the only chance her daughter had. Kate propped herself on the swimming platform and swung her legs into the water. If she looked at Ryan, she wasn't sure if she could do what was needed. Kate pushed off with her arms and plunged beneath the surface.

DAY NINE, LATE
AFTERNOON

C old settled into Kate's bones as the shock of ice water surrounded her. This far out, the ocean's depth kept the water colder. The
sound of her heart exploded in her ears. She shot back to the surface for
air and checked on Ryan. Her daughter faced the starboard side, her
focus fully on the shark.

"Is it still attached to the lines?" Kate shouted to get her attention.

Little head nods were her answer. Ryan's fear made her incapable of verbal communication, and Kate understood. She was surprised her daughter had held it together for so long. It was now or never.

Following several deep breaths, Kate dove deep to get under the boat. Using her arms to give her more depth, she glanced at the hull as she swam beneath it. There were visible dents but she couldn't see the damage that was allowing water into the engine compartment. She swam on, it was too late for the yacht.

The shark's body loomed ahead of her. He was enormous. The perspective from the deck didn't do him justice. His white underbelly merged with the gray upper body and looked to be painted freehand. Their yacht was sixty feet long, and the shark was easily one-third that size which made her recalculate his length. He might be a twenty footer. Scars marred his skin giving testament to his age and his battles for survival.

She swam deeper, thankful for all the hours she'd spent in pools doing physical therapy. Her legs drifted behind her as her long, powerful arms pulled against the water, and she moved forward. She had almost passed beneath the shark when it noticed her. One dark eye focused.

He reacted and hit the yacht again trying to get loose. He'd recognized her and kept her in his peripheral as he fought. With a powerful pull of her arms, Kate shot forward looking for the chain. She saw a flash in the water and went deeper. Her lungs screamed for air. She refused to go up until she had the chain in her hand. Finally, her hand connected, and she grasped the cold metal as tightly as she could. With no air in her lungs, she went deeper, her vision blurred, and her chest craved air so badly it hurt. She reached the rope attached to the end of the chain and used everything she had to gain the surface. He twisted and lunged in her direction as she flew upward. Another spear snapped. Kate's brain only saw the huge open jaws with rows of teeth reaching for her.

She hit the surface about four yards from the shark. Kate sucked in several deep breaths before she went under again. Her eyes remained glued to the shark to be sure it was still secure. She swam deeper and passed below it and then beneath the boat. When the shark was behind her, she refused to turn and look. How many cables were holding him? She surfaced.

"He's breaking away," Ryan screamed.

Kate grabbed the swim platform and hauled her wet body on board. They didn't have time to start over. She had to secure him right now.

"Take the rope and don't drop it," Kate said as she handed it to Ryan.

Kate dragged herself across the platform and grasped her wheelchair. Faster than she'd ever accomplished it, she hefted herself into the seat not caring that her arms were screaming from everything she'd put them through. She frantically sucked in air.

"Mom?" Ryan asked.

Kate lifted her hand and smiled. "Hand me the rope," she wheezed.

Ryan gave her the soggy material. Kate wheeled slowly to the port side, the list making it nearly impossible. When she could grasp the middle rail, she circled the rope once around the upper rail, and began pulling. Ryan helped, and they quickly came to the chain. The yacht shook from the force of the fighting shark. With the chain in her lap, she wheeled to the starboard side and struggled to get closer to the shark.

"Come on," she groaned as she gave it everything she had and traveled on the unsteady surface that wanted to pitch her into the water again. Once she was in place, she tied the end of the chain to a cleat. As the shark's ability to move were curtailed, it thrashed harder. As soon as it rested, Kate tightened the chain on the cleat until the chain around the shark was as snug as she could make it.

"Grab me another spear from the container," Kate yelled.

She lifted the speargun into her lap and waited for Ryan.

"There's only one," Ryan said when she ran back to her mom.

Kate quickly cut and tied a cable to one of the spears and the end to an unused T-bracket. She slid the spear into the chamber, pulled and attached the rubber, and took aim. The shark went still, and she hit the dorsal fin, lower than the earlier strike. The yacht groaned, and they listed to the starboard side with a grinding noise. They were taking on water quickly now.

Kate tightened the attached cord and then the chain. She leaned through the rail and grabbed a section of the net. The shark didn't budge, but Kate knew it wasn't dead. She manipulated the net as far over the shark's head as she could without falling into the water on top of it.

The shark exploded upward and splashed back down before it went into an extended rage. The sudden force of the action caused the yacht to groan again. Kate knew the sound. Anyone who had spent months at sea dreaded what it meant.

When the shark went still again, she was ready. She circled the chain as tightly as possible around the cleat, which secured it more firmly around the middle of the shark's body. She carefully tightened one of the spear lines but the yacht tilted too much to tighten the others.

"We need to get to the life raft," Kate yelled. If she were thrown onto the shark, it would kill her. Another groan, and the boat sank lower into the water, almost going completely to its side. The wheelchair stopped her from moving up the steep deck. She rapidly scrambled from the chair and dragged herself each agonizing foot away from the shark.

"Undo your safety line and hold onto the rail," she told Ryan. Kate made it to her daughter, sat up and grabbed the canvas bag holding the raft. She grunted as she pushed it closer to the water. The way the yacht listed so high on the port side meant they would need to go into the ocean to gain entry to the raft.

She pushed the canvas through the rungs of the rail while holding the cord that inflated it. Once it was through, she pulled until she met resistance. At that point, she gave it a firm tug which activated the canisters that filled the raft's compartments with air.

The raft hung halfway off the side of the boat as it inflated. Kate fed out the line and the raft hit the water. The shark thrashed again, but the water level was too high, and the yacht too heavy. It stopped after a few seconds.

"Come here," she told Ryan, who moved closer. "Sit down beside me."

Ryan, with pure trust in her mother, innocently moved next to her. Kate grabbed hold of her daughter tightly and without a word, rolled beneath the railing. The rope holding the raft came with them, and they landed with a splash in the water. Ryan came up screaming.

"It's okay, it's okay," Kate repeated to try and calm her. "Up you go," she said situating Ryan at the opening. Kate needed her arms to tread water, so she sank as she pushed Ryan upward into the raft.

"Take my arms and help me in," Kate said when her head was above the surface again.

Ryan continued sobbing, but she grabbed Kate and tried to help her into the raft. Kate's arms were at the breaking point, or so it felt. She didn't have enough energy to pull herself up and on board.

"Mommy, the shark," Ryan yelled.

Kate sank beneath the water and spun around. She peered beneath the boat, expecting it to come at her from below. She saw movement as the yacht rocked. The shark was still attached to the yacht, but it was doing everything it could to get away. Kate came up and looked into her daughter's terrified eyes.

"I'm going to push the raft further from the boat," Kate said.

She tugged with one hand and swam with the other. She was past the point of exhaustion, and she didn't think she would make it into the raft. Ryan let out a blood curdling scream and Kate wondered if she would feel anything before she died.

DAY NINE, LATE
AFTERNOON

Ryan, at the end of her rope, had freaked out, and thankfully, the shark was still caught by the lines and the chain.

"Mommy, get in, please," Ryan begged, and hiccupped from crying.

"A little farther," Kate said. She took them a hundred feet from the yacht before she was ready to try and get in.

"I'll need your help," she told Ryan. "You pull, and I'll lift."

It wasn't easy with the floppy siding of the raft, but Kate finally managed to spill inside the yellow circle. She lay on the bottom and sucked air into her lungs and thought about what she had to do next. They weren't out of danger.

When the raft inflated, it activated a light on the top and one inside. Kate needed to turn them off and conserve energy so they could use them at night if they were still in the ocean.

"Grab a bottle of water from the canvas bag on that side," Kate said once she could speak. Ryan rummaged inside the bag.

"Can I have a power bar?" Ryan asked, her tears drying now that Kate was out of the water.

"Good idea. Hand me one too. I need enough energy to use the oars to get us a bit farther from the boat."

Kate sat up, after a little maneuvering, to place her back against the canvas side. She looked out of the front opening of the raft so she could see the yacht. The water was almost to the second rail. It wouldn't be long before the yacht was completely submerged.

She found the oars and pulled the four pieces out so she could screw them together. The raft had a built-in tent-like cover that would keep them from the elements. There were slits in the sides to put the oars through. In the back of her mind, she knew the shark might escape before the yacht sank. Once they were far enough away, they needed to be still until rescue came.

She told Ryan none of this, and she wouldn't unless Ryan started moving around too much. Kate got the oars through the slits and began rowing them farther away. Still worried about the shark, she decided they were far enough out and pulled in the oars. They ate their power bars.

"Come here," Kate said. Ryan looked at her suspiciously. The last time Kate said come here, they went into the water. "I need a hug," Kate said when Ryan didn't budge.

Ryan scrambled across the bottom of the raft and her small arms circled Kate's neck and squeezed.

"Is the shark dead?" Ryan asked, anger at her mom still prevalent in her tone.

"It's dying," Kate said.

"Can I say my word?"

Kate had to bite her lip to keep from laughing. She knew if she started, it would turn into tears that would turn into hysterics. She was weary to the bone. Her head throbbed and she hurt all over. She ached to the tips of her toes, and it wasn't an exaggeration.

Ryan lifted her hand and gave Kate the water that she was holding. She took a long drink and realized the headache was possibly caused by dehydration.

"Thank you, and yes, you may say the word," Kate said when she pulled the bottle from her lips.

"Can I say it loud?" Ryan asked, her expression one of serious concentration.

"The louder the better," Kate assured her.

Ryan took a deep breath and yelled, "Shitty shark," at the top of her lungs.

Kate chuckled. "Do you feel better?" she asked.

Ryan's expression changed again, and her face scrunched up. "Daddy's not coming back, is he?"

Even though it was a question, the words were so final. Kate hugged her closer and ran her fingers over her daughter's hair.

"He loved us. He died so we could live." Kate heard a noise in the distance. "Do you hear that?" she asked Ryan.

It was a helicopter. Kate peered through the opening to see if she needed to light a flare. It was flying straight at them. Two minutes later, the water rippled, and Kate watched the yacht sink deeper into the ocean. When the helicopter drew closer, the water around them churned. Kate waved before she sank down into the bottom of the raft. For a moment, she closed her eyes.

Sam should be with them. They should have a chance to work through their problems. He should be able to watch his daughter grow older and go after her dreams. Kate wiped her tears away as a shadow passed over the roof of their enclosure. Ryan hugged Kate so tightly her fingers dug into Kate's skin.

A man's legs came into view followed by the rest of him. He wore a wet suit, and he tossed straps inside the raft.

"I'm Shawn," he yelled over the noise. "Put these on the child first, then put on yours if you can. I'll take her up and come back for you."

Ryan's hands clamped tighter.

"It's okay, Ryan, we need to get these on you."

"No Mommy, the shark will jump out of the water and eat us."

Kate's thoughts had gone there too. It had happened in "Jaws Two" and "The Deep Blue Sea" which was ridiculous because they were movies, not reality.

"It won't jump up and get you, I promise," Kate told her and began attaching the harness. She couldn't shake off the image of the shark's breach when it killed Sam.

When she was secured, Kate turned Ryan so she faced Shawn. He gave a thumbs up sign to someone in the helicopter, grabbed Ryan, and lifted her out the raft. Kate watched from the opening as they hung suspended a few feet above the water. Finally they rose higher, but it wasn't fast enough for Kate. She took a chance and looked at the yacht. It was fully on its side, deeply submerged. Kate turned back to Ryan and watched until she was high enough to be pulled on board.

A suntanned face peered down from above and gave her a thumbs up. It was her father and she felt better knowing Ryan was now in his arms. A few minutes later, Shawn was lowered again. When he got to the entrance, he looked at the straps that were only half on, then pulled himself into the raft.

"I'll help," he said and quickly got Kate secured. Her father had most likely told them about Kate's legs.

After the straps were tightened, he used the same technique as he'd used with Ryan. Shawn moved to the entrance and lifted Kate out with him. Their feet hit the water and Kate turned to look at the yacht. What she saw caused her to stop breathing. A huge fin moved directly at them.

Kate screamed and looked into Shawn's eyes. His gaze had tracked hers and he saw exactly what she did. He stayed calm, but he didn't know the shark could breach and kill them.

They inched up slowly and the shark gained speed.

Was Ryan watching? Would she see her mother die like she had her father?

An utterly desolate sadness filled her. The damn shark would win.

Shawn jostled her slightly and gained her attention. He reached down with one arm and grabbed her legs, lifting them higher above the water. His legs came up too.

Kate had no voice left to scream when the shark lunged upward.

Day Nine, Late Afternoon

The massive jaws opened and extended. They missed by inches, and still, Kate couldn't breathe. The shark disappeared, and she knew it was diving deep to give it more height in the next breach.

Shawn frantically waved his arm in a circular motion above them. Kate wondered if the lift had more than one speed. But then, the helicopter itself rose higher, taking them with it.

The shark breached and water sprayed around them. Tears filled Kate's eyes.

The shark didn't win.

She wouldn't feel safe until she was on land, but right now, she couldn't help the relief running through her. She looked down and all she saw was a still ocean and the roof of the yacht above the surface. The shark was gone.

Slowly, they rose upward until someone's arms wrapped around her. She was placed on the floor and she did everything she could to control her emotions.

Kate was able to see the ocean and she took one last look at the yacht and watched it sink beneath the surface.

Someone unstrapped her from the harness and placed headphones over her ears. Kate looked for Ryan and saw her on Greg's lap, wrapped tightly in his arms. Shawn lifted her and placed her in the seat across from her father. He strapped her in and took the seat next to her.

A male voice filled her ears.

"Are you injured? Do you need medical attention?"

She shook her head, unable to speak. She sagged slightly and Shawn straightened her and held on so she was sitting upright. Greg looked at her over Ryan's shoulder.

"Sam?" he mouthed.

Kate shook her head, and tears began sliding down her cheeks.

Her father's voice entered the headset. "You and Ryan will be okay. I'm here now."

Ryan didn't move just held on as tightly as she could to her grand-pops.

Kate leaned her head back and closed her eyes. Her thoughts went to Sam, his smile, his love, his faith that she could save their daughter.

"I did it," Kate told him silently. "You will be so proud of the woman she becomes, I promise."

30

TWO YEARS LATER, GULF OF MEXICO

K ate sat in a low beach chair watching the surf. The warm day held a slight breeze that made it bearable. Ryan's head popped out of the water. She removed her dive mask and snorkel, then smiled so big Kate could see it from where she sat.

"I touched a lemon shark," she yelled excitedly.

It was an excitement Kate didn't share though she returned the smile.

It had taken Ryan a year to go back into the ocean and that included staying clear of swimming pools. Kate's father was the reason she finally went back in. They lived with Greg now and followed him on his adventures. They'd come to this cove because it had a small reef and small sharks. He knew that touching one would be a new high for Ryan.

"Would you like some iced tea," a thick male voice asked from beside her.

Dr. Lawrence Cordova was now her father's fulltime research partner. He'd flown in from South Africa after the attack on the teens and he never left. His specialty with sharks went hand in hand with Greg's stingray work and the two men were fast friends.

"I would love some," Kate replied.

They had spent countless hours discussing the shark that killed Sam. They'd examined the animal's behavior from every angle they could think of. Kate's theory that the shark was angry over the loss of its friend was as sound as anything their combined research could come up with.

Lawrence was in his forties, good looking, and wonderful with Ryan. He and Kate were not in a relationship beyond friendship. Yet. But even Kate knew it would happen when she was ready.

The insurance money for Ryan's Gift came three months after their rescue. Following the sale of her house, Kate invested the combined assets into her father's research. Sam also had a substantial life insurance policy, which she reserved for Ryan's college fund. The rest of the money allowed them to travel wherever the ocean needed them without depending on grants. They made Greg's house in the San Francisco Bay Area their home base.

Unlike Ryan, Kate had not gone back into the ocean. Maybe one day but for now, she was happy on dry land though she still enjoyed swimming if it was a pool with crystal clear water. The one and only time she'd gone out on the boat with them, she'd had a severe panic attack. That had been a year ago and, she thought to herself, she was ready to try again.

Ryan walked out of the surf with her grandpops and headed closer until they blocked the sun. She was growing so fast and Kate hated that Sam wasn't here to see it.

"I found an entire bag of garbage," Ryan said and held up the diving bag filled with what she'd recovered.

Greg's endless patience with Ryan had paid off and touching the lemon shark was a huge step for her. She'd finally gone back in when he explained that sharks had feelings. He'd gone further and said they mourned their dead and the shark that attacked them, did it out of a misunderstanding.

Not that Kate believed that hogwash. Yes, the shark most likely attacked them because it thought them responsible for the loss of its friend but she didn't feel sorry for it.

Ryan plopped down beside her in the sand and her father took the chair next to Lawrence who was back. He handed out the drinks he'd ordered. Ryan's was pink with a small umbrella.

"Thank you," Ryan said with a smirk in her mother's direction because Kate only ordered sugary drinks for special occasions.

Lawrence winked at Kate. "Bribery works every time," he joked.

Kate hid her smile. "What does she need to do for the drink?" she asked.

"She promised to organize my paperwork."

Kate couldn't stop her laugh. "That will take months. I don't know if there are enough sugary drinks in the world to pay someone for that kind of help."

He laughed along with her. Unlike Greg, Lawence wasn't a neat nick and was more scatterbrained. Her father looked up to him even though he was much younger than Greg, which said a lot.

Lawence signed loudly and pronounced, "Life is good."

Kate hadn't planned to fall in love, but it somehow snuck up on her. Sam would want her and Ryan to be happy. Kate didn't look back at his memory with rose covered glasses, but she had forgiven him for what he'd done. She felt an emptiness when she thought of him, but even that was fading.

Kate partially covered her eyes with the back of her hand and looked out into the blue water. She breathed in the scent of the ocean as her eyes scanned the surface.

The shark was out there somewhere.

"Mom?" Ryan asked.

"Can we buy a Sea Doo?"

Kate groaned. Children were resilient and Ryan proved it. Unfortunately Kate would never get the last image of Sam on the Sea Doo out of her memories.

"I don't know," she said. "Your room has been messy lately."

"Awe mom," Ryan whined.

With her eyes still focused on the water, Kate replied softly, "Not yet, but maybe next year."

***

Dear Reader,

Thank you for reading and supporting my work. I was a child of twelve when I first saw Jaws at a drive-in movie theater. It terrified me but also started a deep fascination with sharks, especially great whites. But oh no, I didn't stop there. If you're a shark fan, check out Greenland sharks and Broadnose Sevengills, they're goliath monsters from the deep.

Research on BREACH was a dark hole with massive amounts of misinformation. Even something as simple as great white eye color was so confusing, I hit my head against the computer screen a few times. When it came to finetuning, the Shark/r Reddit group was the best and the links people shared to research was a lifesaver. And that brings me to the Shark Tracker app. Complete time suck and had me deep dive into research that wasn't needed for the book. You can never have too much shark info floating around your head is my new motto.

My concern for the ocean and its incredible wildlife is at the forefront of my thoughts while writing this. Our oceans are at the point of no return. Fishing nets, fishing gear, plastics, overfishing, climate change, and the list goes on... and on... and on... are destroying sea life and in the end, it will destroy us. I wasn't exaggerating in the book. Over 100 million sharks are killed each year. The number is rather hard to grasp and they think this is an undercalculation. I don't consume fish, or any animal product for that matter. There are amazing alternatives and I was successful at making vegan catfish that my husband, the carnivore, couldn't tell the difference. I made it using banana flowers and roasted seaweed. It was flaky and everything. Don't get me started on my seaweed and blueberry smoothie, yum. I'm stepping off my soapbox and thank you for listening.

A huge hug goes out to Tara Skaggs for her help in explaining the finer points of life on wheels. You are a gift to the book world Tara and I thank you for all you do. Now for the next Wild and Free Animal Thriller... SANCTUARY is available at your favorite retailer. You'll find the first two chapters below. For more information on my extensive catalog of books, please visit wickedstorytelling.com, or for questions, email Holly at wickedstorytelling@gmail.com.

Thank you from the bottom of my heart!

Holly

SANCTUARY

Chapter One

Bridge Home School for Girls

Misty opened her eyes just as the man placed his hand over her mouth and stopped her scream. She fought but another man helped lift her and they carried her to a waiting vehicle. She never saw her parents or her little brother. The men didn't speak a word which made the ordeal more terrifying.

Misty had trouble catching her breath after they flung her into the back of an SUV. One of the men took the seat next to her. She immediately tried the opposite door and found it locked. The man beside Misty ignored her until her tears turned to screams. The blow to her face was so sudden that it surprised her more than hurt, but she did get the hint and somehow managed to suppress the next rising scream.

Misty closed her eyes, hoping the nightmare would end. When she dared peek she still sat in the back of the vehicle with only her cotton nightgown and panties for coverage. No, terrified didn't quite cover how she felt.

She looked around the back of the SUV for a weapon. Anything she could use to protect herself. There was nothing. The man who slapped her didn't appear to have a gun. He didn't look at her. But she studied him. If she survived, she could give the police his description. Had they hurt her family, her little brother? She stopped another scream, lifted her legs and pulled the nightgown over them. She huddled against the locked door too terrified to even look out the window. The two men didn't care that she wasn't wearing a seatbelt and they weren't wearing theirs.

It took an hour before she found the courage to use words. "Where are you taking me?" She waited but her question remained unanswered.

The hours flew by, and her terror increased. She must have fallen asleep when the SUV turned and she fell away from the door. Light was shining through the window and she could see trees. The vehicle turned left down another road. Low hanging branches scraped the hood and an eerie feeling filled Misty's gut. It got worse when large, wrought-iron gates swung open and the SUV continued down a nar-row lane. It wasn't until they made a final sweeping turn that she saw the old decrepit three story mansion.

A middle-aged woman, wearing a lab coat of some kind over a black dress, stepped from the front door and walked toward the vehicle. The sour feeling in Misty's stomach loosened a bit at the sight of the woman. She would help. The man beside her opened his door and got out.

"Slide over," he said, and beckoned Misty to move across the seat so she could exit on his side. Should she? Now was not the time to release her attitude so she stayed silent and moved over. The man stepped back and the woman leaned in. She was older than Misty first thought, the lines at her eyes deep and the firm press of her nearly white lips, unwelcoming.

"You will remain silent. Follow me." The woman turned her back and walked toward the front door.

The man said nothing and didn't really seem to care if Misty got out or not. Stay with the men who kidnapped her or follow the creepy old woman. Creepy old woman won. Misty scrambled out of the SUV and all but ran after her. She entered a foyer.

"You will close the door behind you," the woman said from a few feet away.

Misty stopped where she was, deciding enough was enough. "Where am I and why am I here?" she demanded with every last bit of her fifteen year old arrogance.

The woman had turned to climb the stairs which were located to the right, but she suddenly swept around, her hand going to a stick hanging by a cord from her waist and had been partially covered by the lab coat. She lifted the two-foot stick and struck Misty across the face, neck, and upper part of the chest.

"Do not speak." She again turned her back on Misty who had her palm over the red heat burning her face. Misty, again stunned by the sudden violence, followed. They climbed the stairs to the third level. The woman walked down a long corridor to the second to last closed door. Using a key from a keyring also attached at her waist, she unlocked the door and opened it wide. It was a bathroom and Misty was extremely grateful because she needed to use the toilet.

"Remove your clothes and place them on the counter."

"What?"

"I do not repeat myself. This is your only warning. If you do not do as you are told, you are beaten."

Beaten? Misty couldn't have heard her correctly. The woman's hand went to the stick at her side and Misty stepped into the bathroom and looked around before turning back to the woman who was glaring at her.

"I do not have anything but panties under my nightgown."

"Remove it all or your delay will have consequences." The church taught Misty that her body was sacred. She had never undressed in front of anyone but her mother and that had been years before. Her shaking hands inched down to the bottom of the nightgown and she bent slightly before releasing it and straightening.

"I can't," she said. She expected the strike but hadn't anticipated that they wouldn't stop.

Misty cried out and covered her face and throat with her arms. Each ensuing hit landed on her shoulders until she went to her knees, the pain more than she could take. The woman reached down and began tearing the nightgown from her body in between strikes. A blow connected with her fingers and Misty thought they were broken as they continued landing and she screamed. She did everything she could to keep hold of the nightgown but the woman eventually won.

Long fingers dug into her hair and jerked her head back. "Standup."

Misty cried into her arms and the stick came down across her back spreading fire. She made it to her hands and knees, snot dripping from her nose onto the floor. Her shaking legs didn't want to hold her so she grabbed the counter and stood as straight as she was able.

"Remove the underwear, now."

Crying from pain and shame, Misty slipped the garment down her legs and kicked it off her feet.

"Get into the shower," the mean voice said. "Wash your hair and your body. Clothes will be provided when you finish. You have four minutes."

"I need to go pee," Misty pleaded between sobs.

"It's part of your shower time." She stood watching, her feet planted a few inches apart, unmoving.

Misty stared at her, knowing the woman would watch her use the toilet which was more shame than Misty could handle. She pushed aside the shower curtain and turned on the water, stepping inside before it warmed. She couldn't stop the stream of urine that ran down the drain. The water didn't grow warmer and suddenly Misty was freezing.

"Two minutes."

Misty could barely see through her tears but she quickly grabbed the liquid soap, lathered herself, rinsed and did the same to her hair while shaking so hard it was difficult to hold the bottle. Misty peeked from behind the shower curtain. The woman stood with a stack of clothing in her arms. Misty's clothes were missing.

"Shut the water off and get out." She handed her a towel.

Misty dried herself, trying to stay covered while she did it. The woman pointed at the clothes which she had moved to the counter. It was a beige, unadorned dress, with a high neckline. Misty pulled the shapeless garment over her head and the dress fell below her knees. She donned the white underwear quickly. There had been no bra but her breasts were small and her mother had just bought her first one.

"Follow me." Again the woman turned and walked away. She used a key to open another door. She stepped back and nodded at Misty to precede her.

The room was spartan with only a bed covered by a white sheet. No other furniture though there was a door on the side that might be a closet.

"You do not have permission to speak. Talking is a privilege here. You also have no bedding. Everything must be earned other than your clothes and shoes which are in the closet. If you behave in a manner that cannot be controlled by simple means, your clothing will be removed and you will stay locked in this room until you comply. Someone will come for you when it's time to begin your orientation."

Misty simply stared, too afraid to ask a question. Tears slowly dripped down her cheeks.

"This is the Bridge Home School for Girls," the woman continued. "You will stay here until your behavior is that of a young woman and not that of a spoiled child. This can be an awarding time in your life where you learn your place, or it can be a time of misery. Either way, you will be a proper young woman when you leave. Your parents have paid dearly for that promise." She turned and walked from the room, locking the door behind her.

Misty stared at the closing door in horror.

Her parents had done this to her.

Chapter Two

The Island

Simon looked up at the sky, his overly large head going back so far he stumbled. He watched the clouds building in the distance for a moment. Jerry, his boss, worried about storms, but Simon liked them. The cats liked them too.

He lowered his head and moved to the first pen so he could feed Carla and Tibby, the female lions who were brought in together a week before. The bucket he carried for them consisted of horse and chicken meat. It was cheaper than beef, and they raised the chicks on the island, so that was cheaper still.

Carla growled and bared her teeth at him. Tibby huddled in the back of the cage, her fangs showing though she didn't make a sound. Simon didn't really know their story, and he didn't know them. This was important because he tried to build rapport with all the cats and mostly he was successful. For Carla and Tibby, he would need to wait and see.

Tibby came forward when the food was offered so Carla didn't eat it all. Simon backed away so they were more comfortable, though their eyes stayed on him the entire time they devoured their food. He watched them for several minutes before he went back to the hut for more meals. His next trip to the larger pen would require him to carry four buckets at one time. That was okay; he was big and strong.

The problem with Simon wasn't his size. He'd been born with the umbilical cord wrapped around his neck, and he didn't breathe right away. They said it damaged his brain. Simon wasn't sure about that. A man didn't need to know more than his job required, and Simon knew everything about the cats. They loved him, or at least some of them did. He loved them all, even the mean ones. It wasn't their fault.

The cats were rescues from zoos and private owners. Cat Sanctuary Island made its money off people visiting and seeing the rescued cats in their natural habitat. It was all for show because when normals weren't on the island, the cats were kept in small cages and bad things happened. He hated thinking about the bad things.

Normals were not cat people. They wanted to stare, watch them eat, and pat themselves on the back for donating money to a good cause. They thought the cats were better off than if they were out in the wild, which simply wasn't true. Simon knew this because no matter what people called him, he wasn't stupid. His job was to care for the cats, and he was very good at his job.

Simon saved his favorite cage for last. He went back to the hut for tastier food because he liked to spoil Indra. Unlike the other cats, he entered Indra's cage and pet the large head that rubbed against his side. Indra was an eight-foot-long Bengal tiger who weighed over three hundred pounds.

"How are you, buddy? I brought one of your favorites as a surprise."

Indra never attacked his food. He loved Simon and always wanted affection first. Rubbing Indra's head was no hardship. The sleek fur was coarser than a house cat's but less rough than a lion's. His head had the softest fur on his body, but Simon knew Indra loved belly scratches the most, so after the greeting, he sat down beside the cat, who immediately rolled to his back in expectation.

Tigers can't purr, but Indra made deep chuffling sounds that meant he liked what Simon was doing. A few minutes passed before Simon stood and walked to the bucket. He spilled the contents on the cage floor so Indra could eat his special treat first, which was a whole chicken, feathers and all. Simon had found the dead chicken in the enclosure that morning. The hen was old and, within the next few weeks, she would have been used as a meal anyway. Simon didn't like when animals in his care died, but Indra got a treat, so he tried not to let the death bother him.

He walked slowly to the corner of the pen. He respected Indra and understood that the tiger, acting on instinct, could hurt or kill Simon without meaning to. He sat down and pulled his own breakfast from his pocket. It was a burrito wrapped in plastic that Yolanda at the cafeteria had given him. He slowly peeled back the wrapping and waited for Indra to investigate.

The big cat moved with grace and power, so quiet and stealthy, it was almost like he was stalking Simon. Indra wasn't aware that his size alone intimidated people. He had been a bottle-fed cub, raised by a private illegal owner. The man got caught running a scam, and Indra was confiscated by the local wildlife center. Eventually, they placed him on the island. Simon knew these things because the librarian at the library in the city had read the newspaper article about Indra to him. It was also why he knew the tiger's name and what it meant. Indra was named after the Hindu god of thunder and war, a fitting name for the goliath beast with the heart of the most precious golden retriever.

With the help of the librarian, Mrs. Miller, Simon was learning to read. Most words were still too difficult, and even when he slowly sounded them out, they didn't make sense. He knew one day he would understand more and Mrs. Miller told him to be patient with himself.

Simon had to keep his attempts to read a secret. Jerry didn't want him to learn anything other than caring for the cats and if he knew Simon might read someday, Jerry would fire him. If that happened, Simon didn't know what he would do. The animals needed him.

He tore a small piece of his burrito off and offered it to Indra. The cat sniffed before he delicately removed it from Simon's fingers.

"You have your own, so go eat it," he told the old cat. Indra was eleven, and tigers in captivity only lived between fifteen and twenty years.

Indra wandered back to his food and began eating his surprise first, just how Simon knew he would. The cat was always curious about what Simon ate, but he only needed a taste to know the food on the ground was better.

When Simon finished his meal, he stood slowly and walked to the door of the cage. He never approached Indra when he ate. He looked at his left hand where three fingers were missing and tried not to think about the pain or the infection that had kept him in bed for weeks. Simon had placed his hand through the bars to pet a male lion named Cleveland. He hadn't been paying attention to the lion's agitation and had no idea that one of the females in the next pen had gone into heat.

In the wild, Cleveland would have followed the female around until she allowed him to mate with her. The male lion's frustration from being kept away from her was very real and it cost Simon his fingers. Good lessons worked like that, and he paid closer attention now, no matter what was going on in the rest of the sanctuary.

Simon turned the corner of the long trail and stopped.

"You weren't in the pen with that animal again, were you?" Jerry yelled, his face reddening.

Simon looked down at his feet, not meeting the other man's eyes. "No sir, Mr. Jerry. Through the bars, like you showed me."

Jerry continued to stare for a moment but Simon knew he hadn't seen him.

"Be sure it stays that way," Jerry finally said. "I'm watching the weather and there's a tropical storm building to the south of us. Be sure the animals are secure. If the storm passes in time, we'll have a big weekend."

To Jerry, they were always just animals. He didn't take time to learn their names or make friends with any of them. He cared about money and breaking rules. When inspectors came to the island, Simon wasn't allowed to speak to them. He overheard Jerry telling one man that Simon was deaf and dumb. It had made him sad that Jerry would lie about him. That had been years ago, but it made Simon want to be smarter, which was why he was trying to read. Mrs. Miller told him the books he needed and they came with cassette tapes. He'd sneaked them to the island and hid them in his room, which was built onto the hut where the food was kept.

Mrs. Miller also gave him novels on tape for adults. He couldn't read the books yet, but he liked the stories and he learned about the world. He liked espionage thrillers the most, but he'd also listened to James

Herriot and learned about caring for different animals. If Simon could be anything he wanted to, he would be a veterinarian.

At night, Simon struggled through the words in story books made for children. He tried not to cry in frustration. One day he would be smart, he promised himself.

Simon lifted his head and looked into Jerry's eyes. "I always make sure the animals are secure," he lied.

Releases 7/23/24

Printed in the USA
CPSIA information can be obtained
at www.ICGtesting.com
LVHW012358170924
791307LV00014B/574

9 781946 256478